The Lass at the End
of the Road

by Libeth Tempero

Printed in the United States of America

ISBN: 978-1-7352431-0-8

Also available in Kindle eBook

Dedicated to the one million Irish who perished in the Great Potato Famine of 1845-1852.

And to my great great great grandmother who escaped the fate of so many.

Chapter 1:
Potato Famine Ireland
1848

I am not dead. I lift my head to see the strands of my long black hair mixed with Padraig's golden curls in the boggy water, my sweet brother's mouth green from eating grass. The mists hid the end of the road.

"Padraig wake up. You have to move, you can't leave me by myself. Mama and the babies are dead, don't leave me. We must rise, fight those who want to ruin us. Queen Victoria with her evil magic, who turned our potatoes into black slime. You cannot leave me alone. I am sorry to lead you down this false road, it is my fault we fell into this mess."

I push my head higher. The smell of the grave is here. Cold thick mist seems to want to swallow us. Your fingers fold on themselves like the corpses by the road. "No! No! You cannot be dead."

Freezing water and muck clutch me. The filth is in my mouth. My cough goes on until my throat is raw. No longer even hungry though it has been days since we ate.

"If you get up, you can walk." Says a calm voice.

God? No one is here with me, yet I hear it. It is You.

I ooze along like a snail. The bog barely supports me. One arm out. The other leg. Rest. Sleep. No sleep! Move! Other hand. Pull long skirts to free my foot. At last, I reach the pile of rocks meant to make the rest of this road. Never used. So cold. This is a dream. No, too much pain.

Birds. I can get in my pallet on the floor, home is nice. Gulls on the cliffs. Not home. No cliffs. Black crows, "Stay away from my brother!" I throw some pebbles. They fly away. Push on rocks. Stand.

"Padraig go with God. I have to leave. Did you hear the voice?"

Curse this false road. Nothing around but hills. No more rocks. Spongy turf sways with each step. If I fall now, can I get up? Does it matter if I do? Padraig is dead. I thought I was so smart.

Our baby sister's fingers looked like his. "The cold killed you, Bridie." I pray you are safe in heaven. Mother Mary protect her. Christ protect her. God receive her. We put you in sacred ground in a real coffin. Mama, I wish you were here. You could find a coffin for Padraig.

There is no one around to ask for help, just the remains of a cottage. It looks like ours after the constables took the battering ram and beat the walls down. I wonder if the day was as cold for them. Bridie would still be alive if it was warmer, if we had found someplace to stay besides the Cliffs of Moher. Why is this happening?

The scent of turf jerks me back. My wet skirt wraps around my legs. Mama would shout at me if she saw me kilt up my skirt this high. No. Mama is gone.

I ache for our cottage. Da played his fiddle as Mama, holding baby Bridie on her hip, would cook. Padraig, Sean, Ian and I would stay out of her way. We were always safe and warm gathered around the peat fire when the icy winds came off the Atlantic.

No more. Never safe again. Tears mix with the mist.

The wind sounds like Da as he played. He played tunes like "Óró Sé do Bheatha 'Bhaile" and "Máire Mhór". He named me Máire after that song.

I could not wait for the last of the hedge school students to leave so he would take down his fiddle. He loved the Gaelic and our true history. What good will it do him now? What good will anything do? A bush catches my dress and I almost fall. It spins me around like when I was little. Mama spun me and danced while Da played.

Sure, I got older and times were hard. Then she started to wail at Da, "You lied to me. You said we would have music and dancing forever. Look at you now. You can barely walk since you hurt your foot. We are behind on the rent because you do not work the landlord's fields. We only have potatoes and a few greens to eat. Not even a little poteen to drink. You promised…"

I hold my ears, but it does not take away her voice in my head when she would say, "I am going to pack up the babies and go to my Mother's home in the north and you will never see us again."

Then the potatoes turned all black and we hardly had anything to eat. I never knew why she stayed until they destroyed our home.

The knife stabs of hunger tear at me. The mists have become a hard rain which blow my hair across my face and arms. It stings as the ends hit me. I shiver. My teeth chatter. Am I dying here? What does it matter? There is no home.

The sound of our door splintered by a ram made of big logs before we could answer it haunts me like it still pounds. The giant all in blue with shiny buttons growled at us. "Get your things and get out. You are behind on the rent." He sounded like the voice of doom.

Mama said, "My husband's foot. It was injured, but it is getting better. We can catch up soon."

We all knew it was a lie. It had been crushed under a wagon wheel. None of us said a word.

"Time for getting better is past. Pack a few things and get out, now!"

Da got red in the face. Mama's eyes made me think of a storm ready to break. All of the little ones were wailing.

One of the men pushed his way past the shattered door. He stared at Da's fiddle on the mantel. I prayed he would not touch it. None of us ever did. Da treated it like it held some kind of magic.

We froze when the man picked it up. My gasp softened by my terror.

He slammed it into the door frame. It seemed to explode. The huge man started shouting again, "I said get your stuff and…"

Da went berserk. He took his walking stick and pounded the one who held the neck of the fiddle. I thought Da would kill him, but the bigger one was carrying a rifle. He swung around. The butt hit Da's nose, blood sprayed. Da dropped like a stone. He tied Da with rope and threw him into the cart like a sack of potatoes. We ran out of the cottage after them. Behind me I heard the crash as the battering ram slammed into the chimney.

The last I saw my da, he was in the cart, broken like the walls of our house. There was not a single trace of our cottage. It was a pile of rubble on the dirt. All of our things were underneath it. The edge of a quilt flapped in the cold wind.

I can walk. Where do I go? The only one who might be left is Da.

As we walked, Mama said, "They will probably send him to Australia or maybe Van Diemen's Land. No one would tell me."

When I asked, "Where's Australia, Mama?"

"Far, far away." Was all she said.

If I knew where he was, I could not get there. I am sure she meant over the ocean, but she had the faraway look. I stopped talking.

I shake my head to make the thoughts of those times go away. My clothes catch on another bramble, and it throws me. I right myself one more time.

Padraig trusted me. I took him to the end of a worthless road. We were to go north of Belfast, Mama's mother's house. We heard tell that there were make-work roads. Some never finished. It was confusing the day we got to the crossroad. No one to ask, nearly blind from a hard rain and no rest, I was just letting one foot go after the next, like now. At least this day has cleared.

What do I care where I die? One place is as good as the next. Maybe I am already dead—a ghost who thinks she is still a girl. It does still hurt when the brambles cut my ankles. Maybe I am just a girl who would rather be a ghost. I don't think ghosts get thirsty, so I am probably alive.

At home, we always had water and a soup pot, even if sometimes it was water and a few greens. Maybe an onion. After all of the other harvests, there were potatoes until the next early summer's lean time. This harvest there was black slime instead of potato soup. I would love some now, or maybe colcannon. The pains from hunger double me. Do not stop. Stand up and keep moving.

Water! The water is over my shoes. Up the hill, there are stones to make what looks like a basin. My feet make squishy sounds as I walk. They weigh so much it is impossible to run, I head there as fast as I can.

The water fills a small pool. "Thank you, Spirits of the spring." I lay down over the rocks and drink like an animal. My belly is so full it is sticking out. I roll off and stare at the sky. Dark blue-gray, a late, cold afternoon. Maybe I will not wake up.

Chapter 2:
What Name Is on Me?

They never told me heaven would smell like the middle of an herb patch. It is mostly wonderful, but there are other terrible scents. I cannot open my eyes. My arms are locked by my sides, so I cannot even rub them. I must be dead. Is it hell? There are no angels, no bright lights, and St. Peter is not here with a list of my good or bad deeds. I thought there would be someone to greet me at some gate.

A bit of fluff tickles my nose. "Achoo!" Dead people do not sneeze, so not heaven.

A strong arm lifts me. A sweet thin voice says "There, there, my sweet Ellen. Everything is all fine. I had to use the cover to tuck you in like when you were a baby. You were thrashing about."

She uses the Ulster Gaelic. I only heard Mama use it a few times. Mama did not speak like the people around home. Where am I? Did we walk all the way to the north? No. I am sure we had a long way to go.

I buck to get away. Her hand on my chest holds me in place. "What is this about Ellen?"

My maimeo', Da's mother, who hated anyone who used English, always calls me by my Irish name, Máire. Mama despised her, and would say in English, "Her name is Mary, not Máire." No one has ever called me Ellen.

I fight hard to escape until I remember. My family is all gone. Padraig was the last one. He is dead at the end of the road. I sink back and cry.

I wish I could be with them in heaven. Then Ellen might be my new angel name like my confirmation name. If this were heaven, it would be perfect. Is Da in heaven? I hope he is still alive even if they took him away. It might be only my sweet baby sister, Bridie. She was the only one who had a coffin and was buried in the churchyard.

The rocks by the spring where I last remember being are not here. I am on a pallet on the floor. Every part of me hurts and I want to rub my nose. My dream of heaven is not real. Tears loosen my eyelids and I look around.

A woman with grey curls escaping her white cap looks at me as she strokes my hair. Far from starving, she looks almost plump. I look at her, but she leaves me wrapped tightly as she stands to tend the fire.

Then I smell soup. I hope this is not like the many nights when the hunger pains woke me just as the spoon reached my lips. The scents of potato soup, peat fire, and many other things fill the air. I hope it is real.

The potato soup reminds me of the harvest, a year ago in fall, after the usual summer hunger. This year, Mama dug up the black slime where we expected the new potatoes. I retch thinking of the stench but get enough control to not empty my stomach of the grass I ate. When? It still feels like a hard lump in there.

My hands feel raw from climbing rocks. I had to leave Padraig in that awful place. I do not think I could find him now.

My legs, torn by the rough grasses, sting. They feel like they are wrapped in strips of stiff cloth stuck on with some kind of ointment. All of my joints ache, but that is nothing new. They have since Padraig and I ran out of food. Maybe I am about to die.

Maimeo' complained when we visited, "I am not long for this world. My joints ache all of the time."

I was little and did not understand. Now I feel old like she described. She was a very old woman. I am only eleven or am I twelve.

Mama's voice rings in my head. "Get up, you lazy girl. You should be helping with the cooking. I cannot believe you are such a lay-about."

I think in Gaelic, Go away, Mama. I could not move when I tried. But she is not in this room, just in my head.

I hear her say, "That is not the proper English I taught you. Say it again properly."

"But Mama, I am not English, I am Irish, you are Irish, and Da is Irish!"

"It is not the English who are starving here! How do you expect to rise to our proper station? We must act and speak like nobles. It is our birthright, no matter how low we have been thrown."

She is right about everything. I should be up helping. I should not be so slow, so lazy. I should be speaking the English, like in the manor houses, the way she taught me. I am sorry, Mama. I am sorry for everything. I am sorry I could not save you, Da or the boys. My heart brakes because I could not save baby Bridie or Padraig.

The mama in my head does not stop. "Irish girls are good girls. You know, Mary, you must always live up to who you are."

I want to be a good girl with all my heart, but Mama, I cannot move right now.

I turn my head to look again at the woman who has brought me here. She turns from the fire and nods. Her eyes are dim and look strange. It is like she is looking at me but seeing someone else. Maybe, I am Ellen in her mind.

Wherever you are Da, thank you. Mama always wanted me to act English. She would have taken the Irish tongue from me. You fought her. I would not have understood anything if she had gotten her way and forced me to speak only English.

The old woman looks at me and smiles. I say nothing when she pats my head.

She turns back to stir the soup, and softly sings what I think is a very old lament.

"I am alone, I'm so alone.
My mother is gone
and so is my father.
I am alone. I'm so alone.
My husband is gone
and so is my daughter."

She looks around at me and smiles so wide wrinkles form by her eyes and on her cheeks. The words change.

"My daughter is here.
Here is my daughter."

She stops her song and looks at me.

I do not know why she would say such a thing. She is not my mama! I never saw her until now. This is not my home. There are so many herbs, and it is too quiet, no Da, no boys, no baby. I stay silent and smile through my tears at her.

Then she is back at the soup and her song.

"I am alone, I'm so alone.
My mother is gone
and so is my father.
I am alone. I'm so alone.
My husband is gone
and so is my daughter."

This cottage is smaller than ours. There is just enough room for two stools, one bed, and a tiny table. My home just had a stump for a table and no other furniture so maybe hers just looks smaller.

There is a hearth with a warm peat fire set into the wall opposite the door. She has made me a pallet in the the only empty corner. I am glad her house was not torn down, and even more so that she was not afraid to bring me here.

Even though it is not home, it would be perfect if only I could scratch my nose. There are herbs, hundreds of them, tied to the rafters. Some look like they were picked recently. Most are old, a pale brown, dusty, and covered with cobwebs. The dust from the ones above me tickles when it falls like a soft mist.

The smell of the food makes my mouth water. She spoons something into a bowl and sets it on the table. Then she loosens my covers and slips an arm under my shoulders to help me sit. I am eager for soup, but she takes a delicate cup and pours something from a kettle at the back of the fire.

She gives me a sip, the bitter tea makes me gag. Hot liquid drips on me when I lurch away. She wipes my face with a soft cloth.

I turn my head away more to regain my composure than to reject what she gives me. She makes crooning noises and I turn to take another sip. I am very thirsty and do not want to seem ungrateful for her help. Bit by tiny sip, she doles out a whole cupful.

Afterwards she gives me cooled broth from the potato soup. The taste is like the meeting of earth and heaven. I want to drink it all as fast as I can, but she holds the bowl. She is surprisingly strong.

Her house is perfectly neat except for the light coating of dust. It is like she is expecting company. Mama always cleaned extra when she thought someone was coming and would make us help her until nothing was amiss.

The last time we cleaned it, we had heard the lord of the estate might be coming. He made only rare visits to this estate. Someone said he might even want to view the tenant houses like ours. Our house was clean as a whistle when they came to tear it to the ground. Even the garden was the best I had ever seen it.

They brought the battering ram across, so it was destroyed. The footprints looked like they had gone out of their way to stomp on all the plants. When Mama had us look for what was left, there were only a few turnips and one onion. I cried to see the mess.

Mama hit my back hard enough to almost knock me to the ground. "You are the big girl here. What do you think, scaring the babies like that!" I wiped my eyes on my sleeve and just stared at where our home and plot had been. Mama grabbed my arm to pull me away.

I want all these thoughts to go away now. I wonder again if the woman is expecting company but do not ask.

Was it the good soup or horrible tea, something helps. I can sit up a bit now. My body still hurts, but the joints are not as sore.

I should learn her name but hesitate. Finally, I gather up all my courage. In what I hope sounds like her Ulster Gaelic I ask, "If you wouldn't mind, please tell me your name."

She straightens her back. Her dim eyes glare at me. Will she hit me? "What do you think you should be calling me now. Mathair is all I will be wanting to hear from you."

I feel pleased that I know Mathair is the word for mother and relieved she does not hit me. Mama would have, if I tried to call her by her Christian name. She is not my mother, but she thinks I am her daughter. I am very confused.

She pats my hair and says "It is all right now, Ellen, you are sick. The tea will help you get better. There, there, my doll."

I try again, "Thank you so much, but my name is Mary."

All I get from her is a puzzled look. Then she says, "You need to rest Ellen. The sickness has left you little off in the head. You will be all better after you sleep."

Maybe she is right. I do not know what right is anymore. "Goodnight, Mathair."

****

11

As I walk up to the spring where she found me, I think, thank You, God. I can walk now, and my stomach is full.

I spot some berries on a bush and some mushrooms, too. I pick them carefully remembering Da would tell us to be careful to leave some for the *aos sí* who get angry when we do not share. He said, "You should always refer to them as '*aos sí*'. You will hear them being called fairies. The *aos sí* consider it very rude."

When I get home with them, Mathair smiles. "Thank you for bringing home these things. Now that you wander more, I want to remind you not to go down to MacNean Lough. The water is dangerous when storms blow. Also, I do not trust the fairies down there." Under her breath she mutters, something that sounds like *aos sí,* but I cannot understand what she says exactly. Then louder. "We have enough of everything we need right here. You do not need to go down there and find trouble.

"Put on your older cape, it will get colder soon. We need to pick some of the wild herbs this evening. You know, the medicinals we marked early in the spring and summer."

This spring and summer I was in my home on the coast, but I know better than to correct her, now.

"Each one has its season. Who knows how many we will need in the coming year, or when someone will show up in great need?"

I think she has plenty of herbs. What she does not seem to have is customers. Once again, I do not say anything about their absence. I do find it strange, she knows each of the herbs by name, season, and use. Yet, she cannot even seem to hear my name and does not notice that no one has come to her since I did.

After we return, put away today's harvest on a drying rack in the yard, we go inside. She pulls out a chair. "Sit. It is time to learn the names and uses for each of these plants. I thought you would be my baby forever, but you are almost grown. It is time my craft be passed on to my daughter."

She places a dried plant in front of me. I carefully unroll the leaves. "I know this one! Nettle."

"Right, dearie, nettle is generally used for gout. See my fingers."

Her fingers look like branches of an old tree.

"I would not be able to move at all without the nettle. It is one of the safer herbs but there are still cautions. Always be sure a cup of water is given to wash down the nettle tea. For us, the problem is in gathering it. When it is dried, it loses its sting, but we have to be careful to wear gloves when picking it.

She goes on for a long time about both roots and leaves, the dosages, and warnings. My head spins from all she teaches me. Then abruptly she stops.

"It is high time I show you where I keep the fairy salts. They do not always cure. Instead, they let the body have time to decide which world it would choose."

The way she talks about them, maybe they would have healed Mama and the little boys.

She continues, "The salts are slowly stirred into boiling water. I say the Rosary to make sure it boils long enough and prayers over it do not hurt. Let it sit to cool before use. One of the secrets, Ellen, is to always boil the water as I described. You notice I boil all we drink even though the spring water is probably safe. It will help you stay well."

She continues, "I have not seen the fairy who used to bring salts to me for a long time, so these are quite precious." Then she went on and on about charms in the water.

"Are they charms like the old ones used to use? I heard about them once."

"Not charms," she says, "germs".

I think charms make more sense.

Then she adds "I did not know about them growing up. I have learned so much from the fairies."

Are these the same fairies she warns me about who live downhill on MacNean Lough?

She cannot remember my name and she makes cures from salty water. She is either mad or a great healer and I am not sure which. If the *aos sí* are her teachers, why does she call them fairies? But, since everything in my world seems upside down, why not add fairies who teach, and something called germs.

Chapter 3:
The Ground Slips

It is early morning. The soft rain makes sounds like a distant tune. It is so green here this time of year. This part of Ireland is different from the coast where I used to live. No sounds of the ocean.

I miss Mama. Right now, I would give anything to have her tell me to practice her English poems. I hated when she made me do it for hours as I worked to get the English accent right. Long hours wasted when I could have been doing something useful or fun, but I would even do that if she would just be here.

She preferred English. Her Gaelic sounded strange where we lived and sometimes people, especially Da's relatives, would make fun of her. She spoke English to feel superior. She always wanted to be better than everyone else which was hard because we had so little. I have to quit thinking about her. She is gone.

Mathair breaks into my thoughts, "We need hot water.

I get up and put a kettle over the fire. Then help her cut vegetables, chicken, and herbs. I watch as she makes us a meal of soup and tea. We never had anything half so good to eat at home.

"Your recovery from your illness is almost complete. Here, have the last of the soup."

"Thank you."

We bank the fire, and she hands me my cape. "There is still a chill out. We need to go find some chamomile."

She always thinks we need more herbs.

It is darkening when we bring back the chamomile and a few other herbs. After they are tied in bunches and put up into the rafters near the other identical ones from the days before, we prepare for bed.

I would like to forget Mama. Then I could be easier with Mathair as my mother, but Mama is always here. I cry at night.

Sometimes Mathair hears me. "What is the matter, my dolly?" comes out of the dark.

It works best to say, "I miss Da."

"I do too, go back to sleep now."

I know that she thinks I am talking about her husband, Ellen's da, but somehow it makes me feel better to hear her reassure me.

When I wake in the mornings, we talk about him. "Your hair is just like his," she says as she brushes it. "He used to tell me that my hair was like the sunshine and I would tell him that his was like the night, so we completed the day together. Now he is gone. It is you who must complete my day."

Each morning she brings out clothes from under her bed. She helps me get dressed every day as if I were still a little girl. I wondered why she never dressed me in my own clothes. I remember the day I stirred the fire and saw some of the fabric of my dress. I guess she took my old clothes and burned them in the fireplace as soon as she got them off me.

As bad as they were, I could have sold them. Nevermind, she gives me plenty of food.

These clothes fit me quite well, and I still have my own shoes. I love the soft worn feel of the material and the lovely colors of Ellen's dresses. I never had such nice ones at home. I also wear the apron with large pockets for doing my work.

My favorite, though, is the lovely brown cape she gave me as the fall chill hit. Even though it is warmer in the days now I wear it in the evenings. It has a pattern of intertwining green vines

16

embroidered on it. It feels like more than warmth, more like protection from the ghosts that come sometimes during the day, but mostly at night. When I put it around me, the vision of my dead family and all those dead people on the sides of the road vanish like the morning mist. .

We spend the evenings by the hearth. Mathair tells me of our family. How there were the great kings of Ulster and all the battles they fought. I know some of this from Mama, who was also from that part of the country.

Mathair is especially fond of the stories about Shane O'Neil and laughs as she tells of his meeting with Queen Elizabeth. "The English dogs wanted him to change his own fine furs for the ugly clothes they wore. He refused but added, if he were to change clothes, they could dress an Englishman in Irish garb so that both could have a laugh." I love listening to her.

I wonder if it was my grandmother who told Mama the stories of Ulster when she was a little girl. I was going to find her when I got better, but I would not be alive if Mathair had not found me. Now, Mathair needs me as much as I need her. I understand that she remembers the things from long ago but not anything from yesterday or even some of today.

I like it here. Her storytelling reminds me of Da telling his stories by the fire. He loved the Gaelic and the history of Ireland as much as Mathair does. His stories were from around our home in County Clare not the ones from Ulster. I was always so proud he was a hedge teacher.

He would tell me, "So much has been lost and even the laws have changed and changed again. At one time the slip-jigs and reels, the Gaelic, and our history were all outlawed. Even Mass on Sunday was against the law. Much has changed. We still do not get to have our children taught these things in the English schools." Then he would always add with a snort, "Not that many around us could afford their schools."

Da also taught Latin in his hedge school because it is the language of the Church. He told me after the other students were gone, "We figured we could use it to get around the English not letting us make documents in Gaelic and yet not use their accursed English." He was so smart.

Oh Da, I miss you!

****

I have been here almost a year now. I can tell because the weather is starting to get cold again. It is almost my birthday. I have no way of knowing what day it really is. This year Da will not bump my head on the floor like he did all the other years for luck. I do not think it helped.

How different my life is now, so routine, so calm. I am used to being here. I decided I will live here forever and become a little old woman just like my Mathair. This is my real life, the other was a nightmare. Maybe I will have a daughter someday. We can live here, and I will teach her all that Mathair has shared with me.

It is misty this morning as I meander my way up to the spring to get water. The path is slick. I like this time alone to think and to look around. It is nice here.

"Hello" says a boy.

I am so lost in thought, I drop my bucket and have to catch myself to keep from falling. No one ever comes here but me. Remembering my manners, I say, "Hello, I haven't seen you here before. I am Ellen, who are you?"

He cocks his head sideways like he is confused.

"My friends call me Kalen. I do not usually have to go so far to find the berries and mushrooms for my family. There are none now where I live. I used to come here with my parents. There was another girl then. She was also called Ellen. She grew up, got married, and left. I heard she died when her house was demolished on the coldest day of winter."

"My baby sister Bridie died the night after they evicted us, too."

I do not know why I want to tell him, but I continue, "I did not used to be Ellen, I used to have another name. When I came here, Mathair would not listen to me when I told her Ellen was not my name. She is not even my real mother. My real mother died on the road…" I sob like I have not in a long time.

"It is all right." He says. "I think she needs you here by her and it is good of you to help. I know who she is. I visited her many times with my parents. I also know there is no one to help your mathair and for you to take her daughter's place is a gift."

I sniff a few times and then brighten. "I know where there are berries and mushrooms around here. You have to promise before I show you to leave some for the *aos sí*. Maybe you call them fairies. My real Da said that we always have to share with them, so I won't show you the ones I know about if you do not promise."

He gets the biggest grin on his pointy little face and says with great formality, "I promise my Lady that I will always leave some of those we find for the *aos sí*. Your father was indeed very wise."

I blush at the formality, then give him my best Queen Máire bow of the head like I did when we used to play King and Queen as kids. This is the first time I have felt like the little girl who can play grown-up for a very long time.

The mushrooms are growing on the remains of an ancient tree near the spring. He is so happy when he sees them, he dances a bit of a jig. I am surprised, and also very glad that I had not picked all of the mushrooms the day before so there are some left for him.

"You are an honorable girl and a true friend of the *aos sí*," he said, "if there is ever anything, I can do for you, you need but ask. I live just down the hill from here."

Just as formally I thank him and say "I too will remember you always. Thank you also for your gracious and generous offer. I have all I need with Mathair just now."

Mathair and I are well prepared for the winter now and spend our days with the little everyday tasks of life. We bundle and dry more herbs, and hang them beside the ones from previous years. We have food stored for the winter. There is enough peat stored out in the yard that I think it could last for one hundred winters. I wonder if Mathair's husband did all this or if it was Ellen. Somebody has left her well prepared for the cold and damp days.

Each Sunday Mathair says the Litany Sanctorum. It reminds me of what we did at the local church with the priest saying Mass every Sunday. I do not know why we do not go to a church, maybe there is not one close to here.

The Latin words gladden me each time I hear them. I still wonder that she is able to do this and yet not be able to remember much of now. She also has me recite the Rosary daily. I do not mind at all, even after all that has happened, I still love God and the Church.

****

Finally, the spring is coming. I am excited to start the planting of potatoes and onions. There will be more to plant later. I love having my fingers in the dirt. It was some of my favorite time with Mama. The boys used to hide when it came time to plant. I was Mama's helper. We always started work first thing in the morning. She would still be bright, and it reminded me of how she was when I was little.

Without thinking I turn and say "Mama..." I do not have time to finish my sentence. Mathair whirls around faster than I have ever seen. Her eyes are clear and sharp. She screeches at me, "You are not my daughter! My daughter is grown and gone these many years. You have stolen her clothes. Thief!!" She has her hoe raised high. I am startled. She sees me, the real me, not her daughter for the first time. I run hard as she brings the hoe down. I feel it brush my back. I do not stop to look. I just go as fast as I can. She is very quick for such an old woman.

I call back to her as my feet fly. "Mathair, you gave me these clothes, don't you remember?'

"I am not your mathair!" She strides behind me. I hear the whistle of her hoe as she swings it at me, so I save my breath for running. She does not remember.

Chapter 4:
Am I Here?

I run down the hill as fast as my legs can go. I did not want to go downhill, but she is on the uphill side. I cannot see her when I stop. She screams like a banshee. She is still too close. I turn and run farther. I have to escape. Why did I think of her as my mother? I should have left as soon as I was well enough.

The hill gets steeper. I have never been here before. I fall and roll, get up and take another tumble. Bushes grab my clothes. I have to get away! My foot catches under a root and the world spins. There is nothing here to stop me. It is only grasses. Oh! A boulder…

****

It is almost totally dark now. I am not even sure if I am awake or dreaming? The rough surface of the rock scraped my arm and leg. There are little lines of dry blood to show I must have been here for a while. The deep black waters of MacNean Lough lap softly onto the back of the rock. I can hardly breathe, fear clenches me. "Oh Lord, save me from all evil" There is no voice this time.

Stars make a faint light. On my second step, my foot lands in icy water. It makes me shiver. I hold onto the rock then find my way away from it and towards the woods. It is different here and not just the trees near the stream that goes into the lake. I see some lights not too far away or I think I see them and then they are gone. A cottage?

As I enter the the forest the moon rises and lights the trees. They make an arch like doors to an ancient monastery. There is a hush here like it is a magical or sacred space. Something in my thoughts says, turn and run, but I go towards it. Today there is nothing to lose. Once through the arch, the bright light shines steadily. There are many people just my size, or maybe they are the aos sí', who clamber around in the trees. Others go in and out of a cavern just ahead.

I follow them. There is a shimmer to the air around me and it pushes against me, not like wind but more like a wave in the ocean. I cannot get into the cave from the force of it.

Suddenly whatever holds me releases. I stumble into a room. Here the air shimmers. The light makes the drab rocks burst into colors. It comes from the the fire at the center of a hall far below me.

Figures dance around the blaze. Their clothes in every color of the rainbow shine and send off sparks. I wonder if they are on fire, but they look entranced rather than pained.

At the far end of the room below, there is a tall dais with a grand staircase which is wide at the bottom and narrows as it reaches the top. Guards dressed in dark silver capes with spears are on each side.

A gold table at the top has thrones behind it. When I look directly at them, the clothes of the nobles dazzle my eyes, so I cannot make out their faces. On top of their heads like crowns gold sparks rise to the ceiling. They look like brightly burning torches.

The castle walls bounce the lights, so it looks like it is made of light itself rather than the dark cave I expected when I was in the woods.

When I was there, the clothes of the *aos sí'*, which is all they can possibly be, looked drab gray or brown. Here everyone is dressed in the most brilliant colors I have ever seen.

I look at myself and notice my scratches with blood and the bits of leaves and moss in my hair. I shudder to think there is not even a change of clothes or a water basin to clean up in.

I attempt to go down to the fire but run into something which holds me back. It is very strange. I think It will give, but it is harder than stone. The floor disappears just past where my next step would have been. I gasp for breath for a few moments before I can go on.

Around the room are tables set with all of the fruits and vegetables I know, and many I am not even sure are edible until someone walks up and takes a bite out of what looks like a large blue ball. Table after table piled high with food.

I am enchanted by the place and long to find my way down to it. I beat against the wall until my hands are sore and my eyes feel swollen from crying. I try to go out the way I came in but whatever let me in is not letting me out.

Without a glance at me, one of the *aos sí'* hurries past and disappears from the side of the room. Unlike the others, he is even dirtier than me and his clothes are torn. His path seems to be the only way open. Although I am terrified, I follow him.

The hallway slopes down from this room. Once I turn the first corner, there is a strong wind blowing, it makes me spin around in all directions. It is so strong my hair stands out straight and the tie holding it back slips away. All the trash which was in it is blown to who knows where. My hair falls back to my shoulders, soft and loose.

The next turn produces a heavy mist of some almost woody but also sweet smelling liquid. It soaks me to the bone, but I am not chilled. As I continue to walk, it gets finer and smells of nettle and maybe camphor. There is also a scent which is completely foreign to me. The scratches on my hands disappear and I feel better than ever before.

The next turn is a shower of the first liquid. Then soft warm breezes dry me. A mirror lets me see the results. My clothes are clean. Even the stains on my apron are gone. My hair has never been so shiny. This is only the second time I have ever seen myself in a mirror and I look until someone else walks into the room. Afraid someone will notice I am not like them, I hurry on.

The last corner turns out to be the chamber I was seeing from above. The odor of the fire is nothing like the peat I know, more like cherries or some other fruit, yet also of ancient oak. I am entranced and ignore everything else at first.

When I walk by a long table the smell of the ripe fruit makes me lightheaded and my mouth waters. Without meaning to be rude, I find myself at the table with my hands on some of the apples before I stop. Instantly I let go of them and turn. My face feels hot from the shame. An *aos sí'* woman across the table stares at me.

Guards surround me. One grabs my shoulder. He shouts at me, but it sounds like discordant bells, not words. Their spears point towards me but do not touch my skin. If not held, my knees would buckle.

"I-I apologize. I have no idea why I would forget my manners."

Then the one who holds my shoulder points at himself and makes a sound, and then at me.

"I am the daughter of the fiddler who told me of you."

I almost tell them my name, but some faint thought keeps me from doing so. I remember. It is from a song Da sang. Something about a girl giving her name to the Fair Folk and was never seen again. It was the one with a lively tune, and tragic words. He said he played it at a fairy wedding and laughed to himself because they didn't know what it was about.

I want to run. *Aos sí'* are dangerous. I cannot. Hundreds of them surround me now. All the bells instead of words start to sound like music. Beautiful music. Magic music. I cover my ears, terrified.

The crowd opens and two of the royalty descend from the platform and approach me from the side so I have to turn my head as far as I can to see them. As I do, their faces become clear. One is

25

Kalen who I met at the spring. We shared berries and mushrooms. He tugs on the side of her cape as a woman strides towards me. His mother? She is sparking red and her stare frightens me.

When they get near, the guards turn me to face them. She sounds ominous and in a low tone talks with Kalen. He drops her cape. I wish I could understand the bell talk. He speaks so fast it sounds like a jig instead of words.

She turns to me and in Gaelic asks, "What name is on you, girl?" My legs barely hold me up. I answer, "I am the fiddler's daughter." I am surprised when she accepts this and slowly grins revealing teeth which look like cut diamonds.

"So, you are, and he taught you well. My son told me about your sharing the berries and using our rightful name instead of that horrid word 'fairies' the fools out there usually call us. It was my wedding when the fiddler from the outside was called here to play. I always laugh when I think of the song about the girl who was so foolish as to give us her true name. You are well taught."

I am feeling much better and relaxing some when the storm comes back to her eyes. She holds the point of her long staff at my throat and says, "You should never have gotten in here. Our gates are supposed to keep your kind at bay. What has gone wrong?"

Kalen speaks in Gaelic, too. "I think the problem is not with her or the gate. When we were near the spring, I pronounced her a friend of the *aos sí*. I did not think. The magic of the spring must have made a spell of my words. I was just so charmed by her, Mother."

She lowers the staff. The guards lower their spears. The storm subsides to an annoyed glance at her son. "She is charming, and now she is your responsibility. Because of the boon of her father to me and the gifts she gave to you, I grant her one night under the hill with us."

Kalen grabs her arm. "One night on the outside, not one of our nights. She does not need to find herself in the new millennium. She would be lost there."

"Yes, yes, one night of the outside not under the hill. She must follow all the rules and you will not tell her a single one. Thus, she can prove her worth as a true friend."

Kalen starts to sputter but she turns quickly and in a stately manner walks back to the table on the platform where the rest of the court continues to relax. They eat like nothing has happened. Kalen sighs deeply.

He nods and speaks in the bell language. There is much music from the others as they bring a chair, table, and set out a feast to take my breath away.

Overwhelmed, I pick a common little potato to eat first. Peals of laughter ring now, even my ears can tell the sound, but it is a music of pure joy not derision. Some test has been given to me and passed without my understanding.

A goblet filled with a shimmery liquid is set before me. It is not wine or any spirits but a cold water with a taste like it is from the highest mountain spring. Guzzling it seems rude, but I cannot stop myself. If sunlight had a flavor, this would be it.

Even though I eat just a bit, I feel like it has been a feast. I stand, but exhausted, I fall back into the chair. Kalen holds my hand to steady me and leads me into a chamber with cushions on the floor and then takes his leave. My eyes will not stay open but invisible hands hold me upright and guides me onto the cushions.

I come out of a dream of being at home, the waves of the ocean are breaking with their steady rhythm in the background. The rhythm changes now. It is not waves, but the bells. The sound still is musical, but it is words, too. I listen carefully.

They are talking about the dance which will be around the fire later. There is one with high tones, she is saying it will be her first dance.

Several enter the room. Someone takes my hand. "Get up. Get

up. It is time to get ready for the dance!" She is the one with the high clear voice. She bounces with excitement.

Expecting to feel exhausted, I open my eyes at her insistence. I am rested and feel as excited as she looks. She pulls me off the cushion and drags me down the hall as fast as I can go.

Opening a door, she pushes me inside a room. As she leaves, she says, "Just walk around, sit in the chair, do anything you like, but don't leave until I tell you it is time."

"Where is Kalen?" I ask. No answer. She is gone.

I sit in the chair to catch my breath and look around the room. The walls have soft curtains over them. Each has a soft sheen and they are all of the colors of the rainbow. I love them all but the color of the sunset when it comes from under the clouds makes me gasp. It is a brilliant orange that changes to a deep pink with hints of yellow and violet on the sides. I stand to stare at it more closely.

I notice tiny lights sparking around on the material. As I look, there are bright pinpoint lights on me too. The floor spins as the tiny beams envelop me. I look at the brilliant colors but become dizzy. At last, I dump myself into the chair to avoid falling, then laugh. The spinning of the room slows, then stops.

"You are done. Please take your dress as you leave the room" says a disembodied voice. Not like the voice that told me that I could walk. Maybe it comes from the hall, but it sounds like it comes from the ceiling.

I look up and see a dress in the same colors as the ones I stared at earlier. It hangs in an alcove. The woman who I cannot see says, "You resonated with that color." She would have made as much sense if she had said, "You are a purple dog today." Apparently, she understands my confusion and adds, "It is a bit like a perfect tune. When you hear it for the first time, it sets your feet to dancing. This color does that for you."

I cannot wait to get into it. I slip out of my old dress and put on this one as fast as I can. Even though I cannot see her, for some reason I think the woman can see me. I have butterflies in my stomach, but I am not sure if it is having some invisible person look at me or the magical dress.

Just then the girl who had asked me to wait for her pops into the room.

"Where is Kalen?" I demand. "I don't want to be wandering around the halls without him."

"You will see him soon enough." This answer annoys me, but she does not seem to care.

Then it strikes me—we both speak in bell language. Following her, we come to the room with the strange fire. Strange in part because there is no smoke, even though I smelled it earlier, and no chimney for the smoke to leave the room. I am almost breathless with excitement. Kalen sees me, nods his head, and smiles but does not join me.

A very small girl with blond curls almost like Padraig's runs to me and urges me toward the fire. "We are going to do the first of the dance of twelve tonight. Hurry!"

"No! I do not know your dance. I will ruin it, and someone will be angry."

She pulls on my arm, "This is a beginner's dance. Many of us do not know it. I do not." She smiles at me brightly and then adds "You will see. No one will be angry. It will be fun."

I am very suspicious when someone says it will be fun. I think of all the hours spent as Mama taught me to dance. That was supposed to be fun too. Mama insisted that I do it just right until I was crying. When I made yet another mistake, she would yell at me or hit the back of my head.

With time I learned how to do it her way. The funny part was by then I was going to other places and their "right" did not always match what Mama said. It was not a good idea to point this out to

29

Mama.

I cannot resist this tiny girl and join the circle. Fiddle music surrounds us, but I do not see fiddlers. Like the color of my dress, the music resonates. My reluctance disappears, and I dance more freely than ever before. I don't want to miss anything. At first the circle is closer to the fire than is comfortable. This is not unusual as the fire will burn down.

It does not happen in here. There is no one adding fuel, yet the flames get higher and wider. There are shapes in the fire. At first, they do not look like anything more than flames, but slowly the shapes turn into pictures. There is Mama and those are the constables, then it is baby Bridie and Padraig. These are the pictures of everything that has made me mad or sad.

This is very uncomfortable, but I stay where I was put. Then I see a few of the others have left the inner circle where it is too hot and moved out to form a second circle. Maybe they decided the fire is not going to get smaller and the choice is to stay or to leave this inner circle. When I move to the outer ring, the pictures do not feel so devastating. They are smaller, some are even funny.

Tiny trails of smoke come off the clothes of the dancers in the inner circle. I want to run and pull them away from the fire, but I cannot. My warning shouts make no noise. We just keep dancing. Eventually each one realizes the need to leave the original space. When the last person crosses to the new ring, the pictures are gone, and everyone starts laughing. As it ends, I float to just above the floor.

The dance is over, the dancers are leaving the room except for me. It is rather like watching a rainbow fade around me, but I cannot leave the circle. I look wildly around the room. Kalen sees me, comes and takes my hand, and brings me back to earth.

Catching my breath finally, I say, "Thank you. I thought I might have to stay there forever."

"I should have been here when it ended, I apologize but I was caught in a conversation. You could never have gotten away without being helped by one of us, and I was supposed to be watching you. I must leave you again and join those at the table. Are you doing better now?"

"Yes, thank you."

He departs. As I walk down the hallway, I realize, the buoyancy remains in my heart. For the first time, all the ghosts from my family seem to be gone. I never thought I was bringing them to me. I thought there was nothing I could do. I would just have to live with the visions and the pain that they brought my way. I never imagined I was summoning them to me.

It never was the right burial in a coffin in the churchyard which would keep them from haunting me. Just me. When I stepped to the outer circle, it changed me. I could still feel the warmth but in my new position, it did not burn me.

The same is true for my family, I still can feel their warmth and the sorrow for losing them, but I can step away from their haunting me by letting go of my sense I could change the truth by wishing it were different.

I dance on the way to the room where my dress first appeared. I need to get my own clothes. Changing into them just feels right. I have never had something seem more like it was mine and mine alone than the beautiful dress, and yet I know it is not. As I place it back on the hanger and step back to admire it just one more time, it turns into a fine mist. The mist rises to the ceiling quickly and then is gone.

****

I wake on a hillside. It is moist but soft. I open my eyes to a foggy dawn. It must be the next day. The boulder is still here so I

31

have not gone anywhere. My head feels like it is made out of dense rock. At first reluctant to stand, I finally use the stone to help me get up enough to rise.

Everything is green and grey around me, even the top of the rock which is covered with lichen. I could stay here forever. It is not good to run off before this haze lifts. Not that I will know where I am when it does, but I hopefully can stay out of pools and bogs. It is dangerous here, too.

Chapter 5:
Not All Is Lost

It does not seem very long ago I wanted to die. I had nothing—there was nothing left to lose. I was wrong. The change, an unexpectedly fierce will to live surprises me. The questions now are how can I find what I need to stay alive? Where to go? What to do next?

Maybe last night was a dream. Such things only exist in dreams, don't they? Da thought they were real. Whether or not it was a dream, I am here with nothing more than when I first left Mathair's garden. Strange to still call her mother, but since she would not tell me her name, I guess it will have to do.

I do have one thing from the *aos sí'*, dream or not. I realize there are some things which I cannot change while others I thought were fixed in place which I can. There was so much magic there. Now, I need to stop daydreaming and figure out what to do next.

I have the clothes on my back. The dress I wore when I got to Mathair's house was snagged and dirty. My search reveals no holes in this one. This is not a gift. I need to be invisible as I travel on the road. Most people I saw, when we all traveled together, looked pretty ragged. Since I am only twelve and have no adults to watch over me, I think I should try to not be seen. I would like to make the dress into pants and pretend I am a boy, but it would take a needle and thread. I will look for those.

My shift is nice and is not torn either. It is white linen with lacy edging and embroidered flowers. It is a lot nicer than the dress and might be a good thing to barter. It does not show under the dress much, and I wouldn't miss it except for warmth. Other than the cloak it is the nicest thing I ever wore, but if it is a slip or food, I will have to give it up. I also have the apron with the big pockets. I am glad I was gardening when she ran me off. I wish it had been cool so I could have kept the cape.

I have both my water bottle and my digging stick. Each would work as a weapon if I am cornered. The water bottle is made of heavy clay and the stick has a good point. I do not want to hurt anyone now, I am a healer.

I also am wearing the shoes Da said were for Mama even though they were exactly my size and much too small for her. Oh, Da I miss you. There are those with even less than me on these roads. I plan to keep them on my feet always and guard them even then.

I talked to some boys about my age when we were with Mama. They had just taken their shoes off to air their feet and in a blink, they were gone. To take mine off now, feel the springy turf, would be like heaven. I don't see anyone around. Silly, it is just what happened to those boys. You have to keep the shoes on your feet.

The haze hides the sun, so I make my best guess and start walking. I shiver as fog turns into a light mist.

The earthy smells of evening remind me of my need for shelter for the night. If I only had my cape. Stop. I do not have it and that sort of thinking is not going to help. The problem of getting too cold is real. I have to find somewhere before nightfall.

I shake my bottle. There are only a few drops left. The water of the lough is close, but I will not go there. Mathair, told me and I believe her. There is just no way to boil it and to drink it could mean a horrible death.

She said the water had germs. I thought it was silly, but she said no. She would only drink from springs or boiled water and preferred to use both as spring water held no certainty. She told me stories of people she had tried to help. They sounded like they got sick like Mama and my brothers did.

"Every once in a while," she said, "I could save them with boiled water and the salts. If they could keep just some of it down, it worked much of the time."

I wished I had some when I found Mama.

I do not have any way to boil water. I have to climb the hill here and see if there is a spring high enough to have no beasties. I would love to find one which is carefully tended like Mathair's with rocks surrounding it, but any would do so long as it is high enough to be away from people. Strange. Where are all the people? But then, Mathair warned me not to go near this lough.

This hill is almost too steep to climb, I slide back often. My heart jumps out of fear every time. At last, I reach saplings and bushes to hold my feet.

Several of the herbs Mathair taught me how to use in healing grow here. I use my stick to dig the roots, then pick leaves and flowers of other plants. This is something else I might use to barter. I just hope I can do it right.

The bushes over there seem thicker. Possibly, it shows where a spring starts. Maybe I can find mushrooms here, and berries, too.

I will need to find a road soon to find anyone to barter with. It scares me to join others when I have no one to protect me. Many desperate people would do anything to get by. I have to go down there to find someone who needs my cures. I fill my pocket with herbs. Will anyone want to give up the food they have to trade for medicinal herbs?

The bushes here are dense, I stop and kilt up my skirts, so they do not get caught. Not very lady like, but not having to stop every other step is worth it. Besides, I am no lady. My dress looks more like a beggar's now.

Here it is! The spring starts in the middle of this thicket. First, I lay on my belly. While the brambles poke my legs, I drink until my stomach feels tight as a water skin. It is fresh and cold. Even though it has a bit of a mossy taste, it is delicious. Then, I dig a hole, wait for the dirt and moss to settle then fill my bottle.

I would love to stop here and take a nap. There is no time. I am starving. The food with the *aos sí'* has left me even more hungry. Still, should I give up on more food? Wait, I see mushrooms and some berries over there. The berries have barely ripened, and at home, I would never eat them. I gobble all but a few now.

The mushrooms are delicious. My hand reaches for the last few. "Stop this instant." I say out loud. "Remember the *aos sí'* have been your friends. Do not take what is theirs." I remember their palace and the fire. Could it have been real? I would like it to be.

I trudge up the hillside to see where I am and where to go from here. I believe, this is the Shannon River below.

I remember the maps Da would draw in the dirt of the floor at home. He had been everywhere and the memory of what he said is the best guide I have now.

He told us, "The Shannon, splits Ireland from near the north to here at Kilrush where it meets with the ocean." and then he would ask, "And what ocean is this?"

I knew the answer but was not allowed to talk during lessons in deference the boys who paid, unless no one answered. Then he would point to me and I would say, "The Atlantic." Oh, Da, where are you now?

Shake off the past. The valley curls below me. There, it has to be the mouth of the Shannon. He called it Shannon's Pot.

I remember first seeing the other end of the Shannon from the top of Bunratty Castle. The whole family were on our way to

Uncle's wedding.

Da took me to with him to go into the castle guided by an old friend. Mama made Padraig stay with her at his cottage. Padraig was so mad his face turned red. I laughed inside but didn't let Mama hear me, or I would have had to stay with Padraig and her.

She told him, "I'll not have you gallivanting around and breaking your neck. You can stay here and help me." Da looked relieved. Padraig was little and a handful then. Was I six or seven? Anyway, I was never a banshee like he was.

As we walked, his friend said, "It has been deserted for about 50 years. It is kept locked up now. However, since my family used to be the kings here, I know of the secret entrance."

Da looked excited. "I have always wanted to see the Shannon River from the top of the castle. I had no idea, man, that you knew how to get into it. I would have been after you to go up there from the day I met you."

I was secretly glad he hadn't because now I could go with them.

The friend lit another torch from the one he brought as we went into the entrance. It was cold, and the walls looked wet. The stairs were slippery. I shook inside but followed silently so they would not leave me outside.

We climbed until my legs felt like they were on fire. I missed a step and Da grabbed me. At last, we got to a large room. Even though we had the second torch we could barely see. The light from high windows showed me enough to see the fancy wooden beams.

I could hear people in the castle and Da's friend said "We should stay quiet. I had heard the Royal Irish Constabulary might be setting up quarters here. They are mostly Irish lads but not from around here. I don't think they would bother us even if they knew we were here, but why take the chance?"

We had no fear of them then. When they tore our house down on the orders of our landlord, they haunted my nightmares.

We got to the tower. I asked if the river right below was the Shannon, but it was the Ratty River. Da's friend held me up so I could see the Shannon River. We were so lucky it was a clear evening. The sunset lit the water with gold and pink lights.

The next day we crossed the Shannon. Da said, "Smell the air. You can smell the ocean from here." I was not impressed but did so anyway. We smelled the ocean every day at home.

I wish I could smell it now.

The ferry took us across the river. It took a long time. Da jumped off when we got to the other side. "Home!" he declared.

Chapter 6
A Homecoming

Mama told him, "We have several days to travel before we are at the cottage where you were raised. Home indeed."

All of us were tired of the road, even though at night we stayed in the cottages of his friends. It was hard to believe we had to go almost to Blarney Castle to reach his family. I had never seen it, but everyone had heard of kissing the Blarney Stone to receive the gift of gab.

Da told me, "You need not bother. You talk my arm off anyway."

"This is where the McCarthy kings sat when we ruled. That was before the Jacobite Wars. It all ended then. We were cast out like dogs by the Williamites." Da said in Gaelic.

I knew he was thinking about it like it was yesterday. In the lessons though, he had told us it was over a hundred years earlier. I think he took it as a personal disgrace.

Blarney Castle looked like the hand of a giant who died in a great battle, waving its last goodbye. It was abandoned, and I did not want to disturb it even to get the gift of the Stone. We turned before we got very close to it.

At last we reached where Da grew up. His mother, my maimeo, or grandmother if Mama got her way on what to call her, scowled at Mama. Mama, trying for once to be polite said something in English like she always did. Maimeo, spat on the ground and went back into the cottage without another word.

Da led us into the cottage and Mama tried in Gaelic to smooth things with my maimeo. I closed my eyes. Mama's Ulster accent made things worse rather than better. Da finally was able to make excuses for Mama, so there was an uneasy peace. I worried at the poor start we had made.

Maimeo was happier to see Padraig and me. She used the Gaelic all the time, "You look just like your cousins except for those strange violet eyes. Those come from that odd mother of yours." She glared at my mother sideways before turning back to us. "You have traveled a long way, come have some bannocks. Supper will be soon enough."

Grabbing the bannocks which were warm and fresh, we ran into the yard. Once Da had introduced us to our cousins, we started debating what to play. I was so happy Da had me speaking the Gaelic because it was what everyone here spoke.

My cousins could not agree on what to play, but we were there to go to a wedding, so the girls chose pretending we were in a grand wedding. We talked the younger boys to play with us, but the bigger boys just wanted to play with a ball.

When my cousins wanted one of the taller ones to be the groom. The oldest girl told the boys, "We really are part of the McCarthy royal family. It is up to us to keep it alive. When we pretend, we remember how to keep the old ways alive. How can we do that if you boys won't do your part!" Reluctantly, the oldest boy switched to our game. The other boys took the parts the girls assigned afterwards.

I had not really known much more than we had royalty in the family before we started on the trip here. My cousins knew so much about how we should act as royalty, so it made the make-believe wedding much grander.

The girl who had gotten the boys to play insisted on being the bride. she looked up to the sky and said, "Oh no, it is raining, we will have a cursed marriage." Later she heard some birds and pretending to swoon, said, "Listen to them sing, we are blessed. Our marriage will be lovely."

I had not known there were so many things which could affect a couple's future happiness. Someone found an old horseshoe and the bride lugged it around with her through the whole wedding for luck. After the ceremony the girls would not quit pestering the boys until one of them finally agreed to be the first to greet the new member into the family.

"Why does it have to be a boy?" I asked.

"Oh, it is the worst of luck to be greeted into the family by a woman first. The whole marriage is cursed forever when that happens, no matter how sunny or how many birds sing."

"Oh, that would be awful."

We proceeded to have the wedding dance and all the rest was forgotten. Most of the cousins were very good dancers. So was I. Mama taught me. We had a cailie. One of the boys was learning to play the fiddle but he was still pretty bad. My Da was so much better.

Some of the little girls fell in a heap. "We cannot dance another step," they called. So, we all fell, feigning exhaustion. We rolled on the wet moss laughing. I had never had so much fun. So much for being dignified royalty!

****

Da stayed in Maimeo's house but the rest of us were in his sister's house. They didn't want the little kids underfoot while they were getting ready for the big day. I had a little trouble sleeping because my cousin kicked in her sleep.

I got up early enough to see Mama getting up. I don't think she slept well either. She already looked angry. I decided to be on my best behavior and try to stay out of her way as much as possible.

Auntie Erin must have seen what I saw. "Would you want a bit of the hair of the dog, this bright morning, dearie?" She asked Mama.

Mama looked a bit brighter and held up her cup like a beggar.

Auntie Erin was one of those women who seemed to be happy all the time. She bubbled on, "It is the perfect day for a wedding. The sun is shining and if our bride does not hear the birds it is because she is not awake yet. It could not be a more fortunate day. Your uncle is a lucky man. I hope they are even half as blessed as my man and I have been."

Auntie Erin is my favorite aunt already. I decided I would stay as close to her as I could all day. It was good to have someone else around when Mama was in one of her moods. The drink helped a little, but Mama still seemed upset. I guessed it was about the way Maimeo treated her when we first came. Mama tried to pretend there was nothing wrong, but I knew.

Everyone from miles around and all the family crowded into the pews. The bride, radiant with her braided hair and blue dress looked like a princess. I snuggle next to Auntie Erin in the middle of the pew. Padraig was next to me with Mama on the aisle. I had trouble seeing the bride coming and wished I could have been on the aisle, but we were close to the front of the church. Padraig and I saw everything once the ceremony started. He had trouble sitting still. There had been other marriages in the family, but I never got to go to one before, so I squirmed a little, too.

I thought it would just be a ceremony, but it was a full Mass and a wedding. They were finally done and turned around. Da walked up to be the first to welcome her into the family. Mama leapt from her seat and pushed Da out of the way and kissed the bride. Everyone gasped, and Auntie Erin grabbed my arm and whispered, "What is she thinking?"

Horrified, I knew. Mama's revenge for being snubbed by Maimeo was to curse their wedding out of spite. Did she get some more of the drink? There was a terrible stramash. Da got Mama's arm to pull her out of the church. His face was red which meant he was really mad. All of us kids wailed.

Auntie Erin said, "All of you. Hush now!" She looked at us like we should have stopped it. The congregation settled, and the bride and groom ran for the door.

I felt sorry for the bride—her perfect day ruined by my mama. The tears which ran down her face, matched by my own. I wanted to crawl under the pew like I did when I was little, but Auntie kept a tight grip on my arm. She ushered us out of the church and straight to her house. She ignored people who tried to stop her to talk. I felt like I did something wrong, but there was not anything I could have done to stop Mama.

When we got to her house, Mama and Da were there. The day no longer bright though the sun was still shining. Da was no longer red but shook with anger. Mama looked defiantly at Auntie but did not say a word until we were all inside. Da was supposed to play for the wedding dance but how could we stay after all of this. They were counting on the money to pay for the expenses of the trip.

Finally, Da comes over to talk with us. He speaks softly and has tears in his eyes. "Children, your mother cannot stay after what she did. I still have to play for the dance and cannot leave. You have to go with her."

My heart drops. I was so excited about the wedding dance and showing off all the work I had done in learning the dances my cousins had just taught me. I was going to be like a grown up.

"Da," I started. His look silenced me.

We stayed only long enough to change clothes—part of mine

43

were borrowed. The tears would not stop, but I stifled my sobs for fear of getting hit. I put on my dress which now looked so shabby, I was ashamed to wear it.

Da did not see us off as we left. Mama was still furious, so she forced us along like we were escaping the fires of hell. We went on a different road, the one towards Kilrush. Padraig and I were hungry and exhausted when she finally stopped. He was screaming, but she didn't even seem to hear him. I wished I did not even have to breathe so she would not aim her fury at me.

It should have been fun on the ferry across the Shannon at Kilrush. The day was bright, and some small boats sailed in off the Atlantic. It was not. I just wanted the trip home to be over and everything to be as it had been.

I laugh ruefully when I remember my hopes, now. It never was the same. As he was getting ready to leave, someone ran over Da's foot with a wagon. His brother brought him home in a cart and just dumped him in the yard and left without a word.

I wanted to see my cousins again. I used to think about them all the time. Finally, I was tired of being sad, and stopped remembering them the best I could. We did not talk about Da's family at home after our trip. It was like they had never existed. I had wanted more time with Maimeo. My cousins said she had the best stories about the Irish kings.

When we got home, I told Mama what my cousins had said about being descended from kings. She scoffed. "That is nothing. I am a direct descendant of the high king of Ulster. My family vowed someday we would take our rightful place in the world. My mother even hinted her mother had proof but never said what it was."

Occasionally I would hear her muttering, "Who did she think she was, treating someone from the royal line of Ulster like the worst common peasant? I did what I had to do."

I knew she was talking about Maimeo and the wedding. I think she was sorry about it, but she never said she was wrong.

I still wanted to know more about the kings. She did not talk about her own royal line much when Da was around. After the wedding, when he was gone she would tell me some of the stories and make me promise I would remember who I was so when the time came I would stand in my rightful place, and do whatever was needed to do to restore our sovereignty over all of Ireland.

Once I gathered up all my courage and said, "Mama, my cousins said they were descendants of kings and so do you. How can that be?"

"They might have been descendants of the low kings, but we are the descendants of the high kings. They probably don't know their family was ruled by the high kings. Their parents are too proud to tell their children all of the history. If they even knew it."

Then I started thinking. What had it been like when we had our own kings and queens? It was why I started the games of king and queen with Padraig.

****

When the bad times came, I was not surprised when we did not ask Da's family for help. County Kerry would have been a lot closer than County Antrim, but there was never going to be anything but war between those two women.

I will probably never know what happened to them, but it does go far in explaining why we were living in the northern part of County Clare while all of Da's family was in County Kerry. No one I knew lived so far from kin.

Now I am doing it again—spending my time thinking about the past I cannot change instead of being where I am. I thought I had learned that lesson with the fairies. I guess it is not easy to follow their lessons.

It is almost dark. I will have to sleep in this thicket or get more lost. I wrap my apron around my head and am gone.

Chapter 7:
A Plan Is Made

Down the slope, I see more and more people. I still shudder when I see the places where houses have been destroyed. I should be used to it by now. There are also houses with smoke coming out of the chimneys. I wish I could join them, but they might be starving even though they still have peat to burn. The road and all the desperate people terrify me.

The packs of wild boys scare me, more even than the packs of wild dogs. I shiver when I think of the pack of dogs attacking us just after we started on the road. I wish I had had my bottle then. Mama found some stones we could throw at them. Strange, there have not been any for a while now, no boys, either.

I can do my best to stay in the shadows to avoid the notice of anyone. The berries and mushrooms are gone, and I am tired to the bone even though the brambles were a safe place to sleep. If I can overcome my fear now, I can find food.

Setting myself up as an herbalist or medicine woman is really the only hope. It will have to do. I think it will. I know I do not have nearly the knowledge Mathair had but, it is more than none at all.

Shelter might be possible, too. Da taught us there are some caves around here. It might make a good place to go. He said the caverns are places most folks will not go as they are widely known to be the homes of fairies or even haints. I have already met fairies and been living with my own ghosts long enough that neither of those scare me much. I may join the haints if I do not find some shelter and get some food.

I must find somewhere away from the cave to trade my herbs. Otherwise, the very people I mean to help will fear me because of where I live. I will also need a fire, so I keep warm and boil my water.

"Hello."

I almost jump out of my skin to hear anyone speak. I have been absorbed in my thoughts. When I calm down to look and see who it is—I smile. Kalen, the boy who declared me friend of the Fair Folk at the spring near Mathair's cottage. Was he really there in the hall? I don't want to ask him. I want to think it was real even if it wasn't.

For a few moments I just stare at him speechless. After I shake my head to clear my thoughts, I finally blurt out, "Hello. You said you would help me if I ever needed it. Did you mean it?"

He stands up even straighter and states, "I never lie."

I rush on, "I am in desperate need of your help. I do not want to be a beggar and end up in a workhouse. I think it is still a long way to Grandmother's house with just the few herbs I have in my pockets. I plan to barter for food. People no longer share food because they do not have enough for themselves.

"I remember they used to when I was little, but it ended when the potatoes all turned black. I hope there are still some who have a little and might have a need for a healer. If I can convince them I am their person, or the daughter of a healer at least, I might be able to sell some nostrums. I also need the salts Mathair had. When I lived near the sea, everyone knew where salts were found but I am far from home. Do you know where there are some near here?"

"Are you afraid of the caves?" he inquires.

"A little but not as much as before I met the *aos si'*, well maybe did not meet, maybe just a dream…" Then I clasped both hands over my mouth. Some did not even want to hear of *aos si'* or people who talked like they were real. Here I am with perhaps my best chance of getting help and I am talking about *aos si'* like we are the best of friends.

Uncovering my face and looking up; I see he has a broad grin which breaks into a full laugh. I am shocked to see him, his eyes are sparkling like the sun instead of being black clouds like I feared.

"Follow me." He takes off like a shot.

I struggle to keep him in sight. The uneven ground and hunger slow me. I sit occasionally but then he pops up near me again. I fight the exhaustion and each time get up to follow. I wish he would give me more time to catch my breath.

I am relieved a first when he stays away for a while. Then, for what seems like hours, he does not appear. I shiver and sit down on the hillside, alone and afraid. Breathe. The air is soft and mossy smelling here. I can smell the dirt and some grasses also. Eventually, my shivering leaves, and I feel a weird contentment.

Just then, I see him. No, not him, just his head like a ball lying on the grass right in front of me. Startled, I throw myself backward. His head has the biggest grin I have ever seen. I am so surprised, I forget I am tired and leap up to run to where he is standing.

He is in a crevice. I stop just in time. "What are you thinking. I could have fallen in with you." I yell.

"It is an opening to the cave. Silly"

"Oh. On my own either I would not have found it or fallen in the open pit."

I clamber over the rocks which line the edges of the opening. It is a bit strange here. I can feel the wind like the mouth of the cave is breathing. If my friend were not here looking like he owned the place, I would abandon my plan. Instead, I follow him into the cave.

"This is where the salts are," he says as he hurries along. "We have to go in a ways and part of it will be very dark. Where the salts are, there is a hole in the roof of the cave, and you can stand upright."

"I would hate to fall into that hole! It is freezing here."

I shiver so hard, I don't know if I can go forward. Then his voice comes out of the darkness. "You will have to tie your skirts up with your apron or they will get in your way as you climb the rocks in the section just ahead."

My first thought is Mama's saying, "Irish girls are good girls." I am a good girl and showing a little of my legs in a place of total darkness is not going to change anything.

I know how difficult it is climbing rocks in a long dress. My brother and I did it all the time at home and I was the one who fell as he laughed. I kilt my skirt and hold it with my apron strings.

The rocks are cold. At first, they are mossy. Then we get to a part which is bare and rough. They scrape my hands. Occasionally, the ceiling is low enough so my knees feel like all the skin will be removed as I crawl through the tight spaces.

He turns to give me a hand when we get to the tightest spots but generally, I hold onto the back of his jacket. Once, when the ceiling drops too low, I grab his heel.

If he dropped dead just now, I would have a hard time finding my way out of here. There are several side paths I cannot see, but the air changes direction when I pass them. I keep track of them so if, no when, I need to come back, I will not get lost, but I feel unsure of finding this path in the dark.

I am very glad he is here to show me the way back to the surface when we finish. My heart is beating so rapidly it is like I have been running, more from the terror than the effort.

There is a bit of light ahead. We turn the corner. A large room with a beam of sunlight opens to an amazing view. It has a smaller stream on one side, but it is only a side stream. A torrent of water sparkles across the rocks at the far end of the room. There is a rainbow where the sunshine comes through the opening to meet the spray. I am so glad the fog has lifted outside so I can see it. Getting directly under the hole, I can see stars in the sky even though it is daylight outside. This is mesmerizing.

The spray makes the room icy. I let down my skirts quickly and hug myself for warmth.

The stream gathers in a small pool which has pearls in it. "Those are cave pearls. They are pretty in there but if you fish them out, they just look chalky, not like real pearls. I wanted you to get the chance to see them. The reason for our being here is over there."

We cross the room where I see a darker streak across the face of the rock. "These are the healing salts you asked about. They are not magic and don't cure everything but a little bit in boiled water helps those who can keep it down."

"You know about the boiled water? I have only heard about that from Mathair! I was not sure if I should believe her."

"Yes, it is well known among my family. The water in here, being splashed over the rocks for so far does not need boiled, but most does. Feel free to fill your bottle and drink it but do not drink from the pool directly, please."

I am thirsty so I go back to the river to get some water. The force of it is almost enough to tear the bottle from my hand. It is worth it though. The water is cold and tastes wonderful.

We go back to the wall with salt after I fill my bottle for a second time and set it on the floor. We have nothing to get the salts out of the wall but there are rocks of it on the floor. I fill my apron pockets.

I stopper the bottle as well as possible with a rock. I do not think I can carry it in my hand as I leave. Finally, I hang it from my apron strings, and hope some water remains when we get to the surface.

We sit for a while to rest before we start our way back out of the cave. Kalen leans back against the cave wall. "Do you know why the folks around here are so afraid of this cave, especially at night?"

"No, is it because it is dark, or because animals come here?"

"It is because there is a spirit which lives here and uses people's own memories to drive them to despair. Unable to endure it, the poor victim jumps into the river and is never seen again. That is sad because if one allows the memories the wise person is not harmed, and sometimes is even healed of the pain of those memories."

"How do you know all this?"

"I have lived through it. My family uses this cave for many things, and I have spent a night here."

"Oh, I was hoping to use this cave as shelter."

"There is another branch of the cave not far from the entrance. I can show you. Not many go there because of the stories. It is warmer because there is no water running through it."

Chapter 8:
This May Work

Kalen found my first patient. She is tall but young, beautiful at one time, long blond hair plaited. The unruly curls around her face frame dark and sunken eyes. Her parents stand back, wringing their hands.

"We have food, but I can't keep it in my stomach," she says, "We lost our home, my family brought me here."

Then she starts retching, but nothing is left to come up.

I give her the water with salts by sips at first. When it stays down, larger and larger drinks. It gets her through the fever. I admit I did make a big show of putting the salts into the water and stirring them. When she can hold down the water, I add willow bark tea for the fever.

Her mother has barley and a pot. When I cook it over my small fire, I add some bugs I find in the corners of the room. No one says anything about them. We all share it. I just give the girl the cooking water at first. I only receive a small bit of food for my effort. I am grateful for anything.

After we have cleaned the pot with our fingers, her mother says, "I be telling everyone in hearing distance about the miracle you made. I wish I had more to give you. Thank you for our lass's life."

I set up shop in the ruins of a monastery. It is not too far from the cave. I hope people think of it as a blessed place unlike the cave. It even has a well. Kalen has told me that the water from it does not need to be boiled. I could not ask for a better place. No one wants me out of here and everyone knows where it is.

The next time Kalen comes to see me, he is laughing as he says, "I did not tell anyone directly, just talked about a young but great healer. Not to the sick girl's family but nearby where I knew her family could hear me. I heard you healed her as I expected you would."

I am not sure I want the label of great healer. I am at least the student of Mathair. I am sure she was truly a great healer before she lost so much of her touch with the present. I am grateful she still knew all the herbs and salts and when to use them. "Thank you, Mathair." I whisper. I wish I had met her when she could have been with me, rather than thinking I was Ellen, but she would not have helped a stray girl.

I come back out of my thoughts and look around. Kalen is gone.

****

As she promised, my first patient's mother tells everyone she sees.

A man is brought to me who is as blue as Ma and the boys when my brother and I came back to them. I give him the salts and herbs. At the end, I hold his hand and feel him go. The wagon comes by and he is carried off to be buried in a pit, no gravestone, and no mourners.

No one will trust me now. For a whole week I wait, sure I will have to move on.

Kalen says, "Be patient, this is a good place. You will always have the ones who do not respond.

One day before the mists have lightened, a lovely woman with a slight girl, younger than Padraig, enters and waits patiently for me as I am setting my things on the new tables I made from pieces of the broken walls of the ruins. When I am finished, I turn to her.

"I am Margret, and this is my daughter, Anya. Can you help her? She has been so hot all night. She is my only child. Please."

Her skin is dry. I ask her mother "Is she always so pale?" The woman only looks down and shakes her head.

"I have something that should help." I reach for the salts and herbs and mix it with the water in my bottle.

"Lay her over here."

The spot is one with lots of high grass. Margret has brought a blanket and we wrap her in it.

I explain, "This will not cure her. It will help her to fight the sickness. I hope it is enough. Was she strong before the fever?"

"Yes, Anya has always been healthy. They demolished our house recently—the shock to her devastating. It was a shock to me, too. I knew the rent was paid but they claimed it was not. I have the coins given to us at our wedding. When we were evicted; they would not even take it to pay for the rent a second time. Willy, my husband was not home at the time. Otherwise, they said he would be thrown in jail for being behind on rent!"

I keep watch on Anya overnight. Margret spoons the tea into her mouth sip by sip. She cooks me some Indian corn porridge and helps me wherever she can. It is a slow recovery, and we stay there night and day.

By the time Anya recovers I realize I think of Margret as my mother, also.

"I told you I saved some money. Please take these coins."

She gave me two coins rather than food! These are the first coins I have ever seen, much less owned. I am not sure what I can trade them for.

One late afternoon, I reach behind me to get my bottle. Startled, I jump. There are a wisp of an old woman and a smaller old man.

"Good afternoon," she said. Her squeaky voice matches her size.

"What brings you here today?"

"It is a small thing, but I have not been able to get the medicine for my achy joints for a while now and was wondering if you might have some."

Mathair had achy joints also, so I know the decoction and have all the herbs, everything except fat to make it into a lotion. "I do not have what I…"

Just then the old woman pulls a jar of fat out of her very large bag. "Is this what you were needing? I thought it might be a hard to come by ingredient with everything being bad right now."

I sigh with relief. As I used my bottle as a pestle and a rock with a hollow spot as a mortar to grind the herbs together, we talk.

"I used to get this from a woman who lived a bit of a ways from here, but she is gone now. For a long while she would remember the old ways even though the new ones were as slippery as a slug for her. We went to her not so long ago and she was much worse than we remembered; just huddled in the corner of her cottage with her daughter's cape. She kept crying her daughter's name, 'Ellen, Ellen where are you my baby.'

It was enough to make me cry even though I know that her daughter grew up, got married and had died.

"We did what we could for her that night, but she had not eaten, became delirious and passed the next morning. I was so sad that we could not save her. She had been such a friend and I regretted deeply that we had not seen her for well over a year."

"Mathair" I whispered as tears filled my eyes.

"She was not your mother." The woman said rather sharply.

"It was the only name I ever got from her." So, I told her the whole story about almost dying and how she found me and thought I was Ellen. "I worked for her like I was her daughter and learned all I could." Then I told them about the horrible day when I called her 'Mama'."

"It was not your fault." She said as she smoothed my hair. It happens sometimes and one never knows when. A person who has been very far away for a long time will suddenly remember everything. Then they seem to fade even further away. I am so glad you got the chance to meet her and learn a part of what she knew. It could have happened at any time, and you probably kept her going longer than she could have without you. There, there, child"

"What was her name? She would never tell me, insisting that I should only call her Mathair."

"Her name was Maighread Ní Dhomhnaill O'Neill and was married to my husband's brother. She was a lovely woman and I am so glad to hear she did not spend as many of her last days alone as I had feared."

"Why was she so afraid to have me go down the hill to where she said the fairies were?"

"Oh, that. She had been friends with the folk down there for years, and they with her. But as she was losing her mind, her husband went down trying to find a cure for her. When he did not come home, she was convinced the fairies had taken him and killed him or some such non-sense.

"It was no such thing. He went out in his little currach. A storm blew up quickly and the little boat was no match for it. There were folk on the shore, but they could not save him. The people around there were sorry to lose her as a friend, but there was no talking her out of her notions. We were there when she was told the real story, but it was like she did not even hear it.

"We could not get her to move into our house. So, there she stayed, alone until you came to her. We did not know when they told her, how far her mind had strayed, and were quite confused by her anger.

More tears than I cried for Mama, keep me from saying anything for a while. Finally, I say, "I morn her. I would have stayed with her to the end if she had not turned into some kind of banshee because of one thoughtless word."

"We do understand, and we can all grieve for someone as fine as she had been." Said her husband.

I finish the cream and give it to her in the same jar which she had held the fat.

"Thank you so kindly. By the by, my name is Triona O'Neill and my husband here is Thomas if you need any help, please let us know."

"Thank you. I will not be staying here for very much longer. I am going to travel to Antrim County as soon as my friend Margret and her family are ready to leave. I will travel with them to Belfast and then go north up the coast to my grandmother's."

Mrs. O'Neill then pressed a small kettle into my hands in payment.

"I can't take this. There is no charge. You have given me far more that I could have hoped in the information."

"Think of it then not as a payment but as a small inheritance. It belonged to her at one time"

Smiling, I took it from her. It was just what I needed as I had only the one bottle to serve all my needs. "Thank you. Thank you so much for everything"

They walk off into the night, hand in hand. It seemed funny for such an old couple.

****

Tomorrow is the day we leave. My thoughts are far away as I put everything right and pack up for the night. As I finish, I realize that it is not only almost dark but also cloudy. I should have left long ago. I do not keep my stores of food, trade goods, and herbs near where I am working so I need to get them put away before I go to sleep. The wild boys have been watching me lately with hungry stares. They know of my success and it has gotten dangerous here.

I am glad that I will have Margret and Anya, it will be so much safer than traveling alone. I haven't yet met her husband, Willy but she is so nice that I am sure I will like him. They will be with me all the way to Belfast.

I think that my grandmother is not much farther north of there. Anya's family plans to go to Liverpool in England and then on to America. They told me they might have to stop in England to make enough money for the passage. I still cannot believe that Margret gave me some of her precious money.

They are hoping they might become ballast on a ship, it is dangerous and there is only water provided but they think they could leave earlier if they do not stop long enough to make the fare necessary for a better berth. They are almost desperate to leave Ireland for America.

I think about all the things I need to pack and how to make them all as small as possible. I do not want to seem like a tinker. I look around finally to see myself on almost a direct route to my stores. I have a shivery feeling like I am being watched. It is the wild boys, much to close. If I had gone a few steps more, they would have seen my crevasse and all my work here would have been lost. I veer ever so slightly away to the only place I feel I can find safety, the entrance to the cave with the river.

It is early evening. I would not go there, but the stories I have heard about the boys are worse than what I know about the cave. They come near enough so I see their wild eyes. I drop down into the entrance. Of course, they know where I am, but here their knowledge is to my advantage. They stop. The warnings about going into the cave, especially at night keep them from getting me. Still, if I had another choice...

They are outside. I can hear one. "Come here, I won't hurt you." Which is followed by howls of laughter and a few stones which hit the cave floor behind me. The stones miss me, but the words and laughter hit their mark.

I head to where I have been sleeping. The crunch of rock echoes from behind me. Someone has entered the cavern. There is only one choice, to go back to the room with the river. I can feel a push against me like the space itself is warning me to stay away. I only hope that I can survive whatever is here waiting for me. I can feel it. The boy must feel it too.

His voice fades, but I still hear his chatter. "We won't hurt you. Come join us." It disappears as I claw to get to the back of the cave.

From above one of them says, "We don't need to chase her. The cave will. Let's stay here to see if she makes it out."

I enter the darkest part of the cave just before the room with the river and pool of cave pearls. I feel suffocated. I am safe from the boys, but am I safe from whatever is here?

I feel my way to where I think the shallow pool is, then look up to see that the sky is dark outside, not even a star in sight. My teeth chatter.

Whatever spirit is here, it is no friend of mine. I feel water seeping into my shoes from the pool. Off to my left I can hear the cascade of the river bounce over the rocks into the depths. I say the Rosary to calm my fears and remind me of God.

That works momentarily, but then pain, like I have swallowed a stone, hits. I do not feel sick, just overwhelmed. I curl up on the cave floor for a long time, all is black, even my thoughts. Then something releases. I see Bridie's face, blue from the cold and a single tear from my left eye runs across my nose. My stomach is better, but more hurts come.

I pray to God to help me. I know I cannot be strong enough without His help. The terror almost consumes me. The river calls me to let my dread be washed away in its depths. I keep watching my dead family come out of the dark and continue to pray.

More of the hurts in my body release. I see the flashes of all the times I had to bury my fear from myself. The torrent of water ceases to draw me. I am overcome by peace. I feel supported in this effort. Thank You God. This place has no power against me. Thank you, Kalen, for letting me know I could survive here.

I find a smooth place on the rocks. Using a stone for a pillow, I fall to sleep.

As light hits my face, I wake. The cave is just a cave again, but I am cold and hungry. I relieve myself further back, but I needed to get food on the way, yesterday. I quietly creep to the entrance of the cave and poke my head up high enough to see the boys. They snore loudly so I stand up and leave the shelter of the cave.

The sun has already broken the mists. It is later than I expected. I quietly walk past the boys, but they do not stir. They must have found or, more likely, stolen some poteen. They stink of raw spirits, piss, and vomit.

I turn around often as I walk, still afraid that one of them only pretends to sleep but nobody follows me.
I reach my stores. All of my thoughts of hunger and neatly packing are forgotten as I gather up everything in my apron and run to meet my friends.

Chapter 9:
Gifts Come in Disguise

The road is empty except for a few strangers. I ask each one, "Have you seen a blond girl with her parents leaving here this morning?"

Each shakes his head until I reach a small old woman. She grins and says, "I traded them a bottle of drink for some food. I brewed it myself." She holds one up for me to see. "Would you like one, sweety. You look like you have plenty to barter."

She has an odd smell and something about her eyes gives me an unsettled feeling. With a slight shiver I shake off the hand she puts on my arm, say "Thank you, no," then move away quickly.

So now I know. Anya and her parents are gone, and I am on my own again. I want to give up. One glance back at the old woman and the road seems more inviting. It is made of stone, very much like the road to nowhere, except this one has walls on both sides. Many people have no other place to relieve themselves, so the stench is worse than when we had our pig.

After I drop my bottle for the second time, I realize I need to sort things so I can move quickly. The willow branch overhanging the wall is the perfect place to repack my things and put my few coins inside my shoes. They may cause some blisters but better than to tempt a thief.

I never had actual money before. We always bartered at home. My herbs, the bottle, and stick are now in one apron pocket and my bits of food in the other. With my kettle in my hand, I am set to go.

There are several who eye me suspiciously as I look for my friends. I keep my hand on the bottle in case I need to use it for a club. Thankfully, everyone seems too weak or tired to bother me.

I soon find a large family and do my best to look like I am an older sister trailing behind. When they stop, I pass them and start looking for another family who would not mind a stray tagging along behind. I do try to find ones who are moving quickly as I still hope to catch Anya and her family.

It is a rare clear and hot day. Da used to say an Irishman would complain the whole day about the rain but let it get warm and bright and he would complain just as loudly about the infernal heat. Miss you Da, but I am glad not to hear of your aches, which would have dogged my steps today.

I have to drink my water faster get the dizzy and an ache in my gut. My arms are bright red where they stick out from my sleeves. My face feels like it is on fire. Ahead there is a cottage with only half a roof. I set my sights on it as a refuge from this horrible sun.

Where did Anya and Margret go? It surprises me they did not wait. Margret treated me like the mother I wished I had, and Anya was like a younger sister. Maybe it was Anya's da who hurried them. Anyway, I was late, and they left.

The cottage where I hope to find shelter is farther than I thought. It is almost dark. I still have my mind set on it as I would like even a part of a roof over me tonight. It would at least keep dogs away if the door shuts.

The yard is scattered with muck and the garden has footprints of a thousand bare feet. Curses on all the landlords and constables for throwing us to the roads while we starved because of the rotten potatoes. They did not have to force us out when we were barely making it anyway.

The door is hanging open off one hinge. I am surprised the place is still standing. It is so damaged. I pause in the doorway for a moment and wait to see in the darkness of the room. It reeks of something almost but not quite like poteen and the smell of blood.

Margret is on the floor, but her head and part of her face looked like they have been bashed in and she is holding Anya, who is recognizable only by her dress which is mostly covered in blood. She barely looks human. I drop my pot to hold her hand in mine. It is cold and stiff.

I look around. Who did this? A man, maybe Anya's father, leans against a stump, dead. In his hand, there is a broken bottle with pieces of skin stuck to it and strands of Anya's blond hair. The wound in his throat looks ragged, not like a knife did it. Has he killed them then cut his own throat? It is the same bottle as the old woman was selling. Poor sweet Anya! If I had been with them, would I be dead now?

I barely get out of the door before I retch, then slip on something wet in my hurry to get away. The moon shines so I can see, then disappears behind a cloud. Pitch black. I should stop. The ground falls away. I hit the bottom of a ditch and want to keep running. I cannot move.

****

The rain drips on my face and wakes me. Water covers my ankles. I squeeze my eyes more tightly shut. The air, sickly sweet with the stench of death would gag me if there was anything in my stomach. I open my eyes and shut them quickly.

In front of me is a boy, his curly hair reminds me of my brother Padraig. I do not want to believe this boy is really dead, but his mouth is green just like Padraig's was and he stares blankly. I push myself to where I can touch him, but he does not move. I am sure he is gone.

I lose myself in grief over a boy I don't know. It is light, yet blackness is swirling inside my head. I no longer have the will to move and no longer feel anything but the coldness.

I just want to curl in a small ball and let everything go away. The picture of Margret and Anya plays over and over in my head. The stench of blood in the cottage, the smell of death from the boy beside me hollow me. Anya and her parents were supposed to keep me safe.

The cold of rock and turf beneath my skin now feels welcome. Take all my warmth.

****

Something grabs at me. "Leave me alone!" The hand on my shoulder does not go, if anything it shakes harder. I turn my face towards the wall of the ditch and refuse to open my eyes. The pincher like grip pulls away. Good. I want to die here. Someone grabs under my arms. I fly through the air and land on my side. It knocks the air out of me.

Kalen of the Fair Folk glares at me, then says. "What do you think you are doing? Why are you in this ditch?" His voice suddenly changes. "Sorry. Did I hurt you? Are you sick? I was so scared when I saw you there."

I point back to the cottage and force out the words. "Those are the people. Those are the people…I-I was supposed to be with them." This is all I can get out.

Kalen walks back to the cabin. The shock on his face says it was not a bad dream.

"Can you get up and walk?"

"I do not want to go anywhere."

"You will not stay here. I am on my way to see my cousin in the north, and you are coming with me."

65

Before I can blink, he has me on my feet and we leave. My shoes make squishy sounds. My feet seem unconnected to the rest of me. I stay silent. The effort it takes to talk exhausts me. Mile after mile much of it on paths which seem like they could disappear at any moment.

He feeds me berries which he slips into my mouth. I do not help nor resist. At night we sleep under the stars. He puts his cloak over me, and says, "I feel warm enough. You take it."

Most nights I shiver uncontrollably and get little sleep. When I do sleep, horrible dreams come, and my screams wake me.

We travel quickly, but not because I want to go this fast. It simply takes no work. Sometimes the feeling is more like riding than walking. Thoughts of how strange walking like this swirl with horrible scenes of what has happened.

The world has ceased to make sense. Maybe, this is all a dream and when awake, I will find myself in our cottage with Da, Mama, the boys and Bridie. It would make more sense if it were a dream.

We halt at a very strange place. Kalen's voice breaks into my thoughts. "The folk around here call this the Giant's Causeway. It is made of these tall rock columns. They mostly have six sides. My mother's family lives here. They've kept it hidden from the other residents of County Antrim. We are not very well liked."

"Stand here." He pushes me into a nook in a wall made of the stone columns. He places a hand on one of the stones. It swings like a giant door but makes no noise.

The inside looks like the same grey rock as on the outside. Here they seem almost polished. This place is both beautiful and grim. The grimness suits my mood. Once again there is a platform, a dais might be a better word since the royal family is assembled on it. Unlike where Kalen lived, there are no bright colors but a soft greyness in their dress and manor.

Quickly, people who look like Kalen's mother surround us.

They all talk at once in bell talk like when we were with Kalen's parents, but now I cannot understand it. I sit on the floor without planning to do so.

Kalen speaks as loudly as possible in his small voice. To get up seems like too much effort, I lie down. They crowd me. Then the group parts, and I am lifted by a small but strong woman. The voices, which seem more urgent now, are rapidly left behind.

She takes me to a room which looks like a home of giant cocoons. I think I would be amazed or frightened if not for the grey veil of my grief. A small part of me wants to be excited. The darkness is winning.

A table rather than a bed is where she lays me. Finally, my chance comes to curl around my legs and pretend the world has gone away. She offers me something to drink.

My thirst surprises me. As I suck the straw the taste of a sweet and yet bitter liquid, fills every corner of me. I think of Mathair's oat straw tea with honey. We used oat straw for…

****

A gauze covers my eyes when I open them. I vaguely remember waking many times. I wiggle but cannot move more than a bit. This is one of the cocoons. Where do I remember seeing them?

A voice which reminds me of the one in the room where I got my dress, here but not here. Oh, yes. I remember coming with Kalen to his cousin's house. Life seemed like too much effort, but he insisted. Is this a healing place? How long have I been here?

A weird echo repeats my questions precisely in Gaelic. "Is this a healing place? How long have I been here?"

My sense is, it has been a very long time. "It has been a very long time." Echoes in my head. Drifting in and out of awareness, I only want to drink from the straw and sleep.

67

The liquid used to be bitter, I am sure of it, but now it is sweet. I think sometimes they took me out of my wrapping and moved my legs only to rewrap me.

The absolute horror I felt when Kalen found me is gone, but there is so much that is not right. I continue to ask questions in my thoughts only to have them echoed back to me. Finally, I get to the most important question. Why am I still here when almost everyone I cared about is gone?

Faithfully, the words come back to me, "Why am I still here when everyone I cared about is gone?"

It is funny but when the questions are just thoughts they do not need to be answered, but when spoken, I feel the need to answer. So, what is it?

"So, what is it?"

The memory of the other voice, the one at the end of the road comes to me. It did not explain why I should not die, and yet I knew getting up and walking was the most important thing. This is why I need to live, because I can. Because I can.

The English are my enemies. To let myself die means I would be helping the very people who want to get rid of me forever. I picture constables destroying my home. I know the English landlord would be just as happy if we were all dead. He even made our closest friends turn us away. When Mama cried, her friend said, "We were warned our house would be next if we help you." I cannot let them win.

At this thought, I push my legs hard against my wrappings. I am furious to think I almost helped the people who have done their best to destroy my world. My arms shoot out of their prison. Jerking through the cloth, I finally see where I am.

It is the room with the cocoons. The woman is here. The one who brought me to this place. "How long have I been here?" I demand.

She is unaffected by my anger. "You are reborn today! Welcome back into the world. Our time is different from yours. I cannot tell you how long it has been in your world. In ours you have been here for a year."

I gasp. "So long?"

She hands me my clothes and leads me to a room where I can dress in private. Was I really here for a year? I am calmer now.

"Are you hungry?" she asks.

"I had not noticed it, but I am ravenous."

"All we have is the food of the fair folk and a few berries. You should be careful not to eat our food and not too many berries. You have had no solid food for a long time. It will take a while to become used to it again."

She leads me down the hallways to a room with food. There are only a woman and her helper cooking here. They do not eat anything. Bell talk. I wish I could understand them.

The cook has me sit at a table near the fireplace. I start to eat when I think of Kalen. My guide turns and leaves me with the cooks.

I jump off my stool to run after her. "Kalen! Where is Kalen?" I shout through the empty halls. No one appears. Am I all alone here?

Kalen runs towards me from a side hall. I fall into his arms. Relief washes away the terror.

"I came as soon as she told me you were out of the cocoon. You made it. You came back."

I noticed he did not say I came back to him. My small doubt dissolves as happiness floods my mind.

We walk back to the kitchen. He joins me in eating the berries. He seems quieter than I expect. "What is the matter, Kalen?"

"I know you just came back to me, but you are going to have to go back to the place where I found you. I cannot stay with you."

Tears stream down my face. All the happiness I felt disappears. "You don't like me? You don't want me here?"

"It is nothing like that. Finish your berries. I need to take you to my uncle. He can show you. Words are not enough—at least they were not enough for me. I think you will have to see to understand. I do want you here. I want to keep you safe and happy forever."

"I am not hungry anymore. Show me whatever it is you have to show me." I feel confused and angry.

He seems to ignore my feelings which makes me even angrier. He stands and holds out his hand. Reluctantly, I take it.

The hall we turn into extends so far, the many sided stones seem to form smooth walls. I struggle to go on. Somehow, I continue until finally we come to a small door. Kalen unlocks it to reveal a circular stairway set into the hexagonal space. He enters quickly and does not see the tear rolling down my cheek. The stairs look like they continue to the sky.

At the top of the stairs a man waits and without a word, opens a door, and follows us into a large room with no furniture.

"This is my mother's oldest brother. He has someone to show you."

His uncle gestures to a woman, facing away so I cannot see her face. She is dancing a jig faster than anyone I have ever seen, but her shoulders slump, and her arms seem to flop at her sides.

"I would like you to meet my wife. She is a person from the outside like you are. Actually, I think she is your mother's older sister, Annie."

At the sound of her name, she spins around to stare at us, feet still moving. Everything about her except the sea-green color of her eyes, and wrinkles, make her seem just like I remember Mama.

I run to her and hug her. "Aunt Annie, it is me, your niece, Mary! I am thrilled to find you."

I would have gone on saying all the things I was thinking, but her dance does not even miss a beat. I take a step back. She looks right through me.

70

Kalen's uncle steps in and takes my hand. "They tried to warn me. We were young and in love. She looked into my eyes as she told me she could dance better than she could before she met me. She told me she loved dancing and she loved me, so we were a perfect match.

"It was true. She won every contest for miles around. We came here and demanded to be allowed to get married. Kalen, your mother tried hard to stop us. My father said at the very least I should take her only as a mistress and never marry her. I thought I knew what was right and wanted to do it. She will not die as long as I am alive but each year she dances faster and is further away. She is more like a ghost tied to a place she cannot leave."

"Oh." This is awful. Kalen would never put me through the hell Aunt Annie's life has become. I look at him. Tears, streaming down his face mirror my own.

His uncle puts a hand on each of our shoulders, escorts us out the door, and stops to lock it. "If I let her out of here, she becomes frantic. One night, her screams reminded a guest here of a banshee crying out before a death. He nearly died of fright. Our family has some banshees, but she is not one of them, just a lost human. She is a mad woman and the fault lies at my doorstep."

My thoughts wander. Shee, oh yes, it is the other name for these folks so the Banshees who cry out before a death are of Kalen's kin. Strange, I have heard them many times before the potatoes turned black. There should be a constant screech these days. I wonder at their silence now.

His uncle is still talking when I realize I have not been listening. "Kalen has told me of your difficulties. We would help you if it would not make everything much worse." Then he whispered to himself, "They all tried to tell me."

We leave him in the tower and make our way down the stairs and across the castle. My food still is on the plate. I devour it. We leave this tomb-like place of grey stone without a single goodbye. Someone has put dried berries in my pocket.

"I have been told I need to take you back to the exact place I found you. No time will have passed. The time with the Fair Folk does not match yours. When we get there, I will position you just as I first found you. Do not watch me go. My uncle says we have already spent too much time together. I do not want you to end up like your Aunt Annie. My family says it should not be bad unless you watch me leave. I understand, they are right, but it breaks my heart to have to leave you to such a hard life."

He is right. We have been together too long. I have felt a wildness in me which wants to stay with him. With him, I can run faster than the wind, never tiring, never hungry. This is the same madness I saw in Aunt Annie, who did stay too long with Kalen's uncle. I walk silently all the way to the edge of the ditch—not trusting what might come out of my mouth.

The dead boy is still where he was. I lay myself on the rocks and turf next to him then shut my eyes. Kalen moves my arms and legs, until they are just like they were. He scrambles out of the ditch. I wait for the silence to let me know he is gone. This time, forever. I am truly alone.

Chapter 10:
The Road Goes On

I set my mind on thoughts of my grandmother's house to close out everything else. My legs feel like they are made of clay—not living. It takes all my effort just to move. I miss Kalen's magic already.

Food, there is a family cooking near the road and the smells are a reminder of the last time my whole family ate together. The stench of cooked rotten potatoes still gags me. There is no reason to stop and cook even if I had the stomach for it. I still have water and the berries I found in my pocket when we left the Giant's Causeway.

I have a moment's gratitude when I remember this and the other things the Fair Folk gave me. I have another when I realize, because I ran in the dark, the fall could have broken my bones.

Grief hits unexpectedly. Mathair's kettle! I dropped it when I held Anya's hand at the cottage. I could go back—no, as much as it means to me, I cannot face them again.

There are so many people on the road here. The old man next to me looks like he is only bones. He wavers and bumps into me. I feel his bones against my own. How does he keep going? How do any of us keep going?

So many of these people are near starvation. The tiny children are the worst. Naked or almost so, with none of the soft roundness that Bridie… I dare not go there if I am going to continue. The past drags at me.

I wish there were enough to feed everyone. Many are coughing. I do my best to make it look like I cough to hide my food as I eat.

When Mama was with us there were generous people in some places, now nothing for anyone. People are catching rats, bugs, and sneaking into fields to drink the blood of cattle, sheep, and pigs.

Ahead are parents with a very young girl and her three brothers. Their mother drags the girl. She clearly does not have enough strength to carry her. The tiny girl cries and reaches out her other hand to be picked up.

"Can I help you with the wee one?"

At first the mother eyes me like I would like to spirit the girl away, but then she seems too exhausted to care. She turns her towards me. "Thank you for your help."

"My name is Deirdre, and the wee lass there is Maebh. Shamus, my husband is over there, and these young ruffians are Tommy and Kelley."

I look down at the girl and smile. "Maebh starts with the same letter as my name, Máire but sometimes I go by Mary. My da was a teacher. He insisted on the Gaelic while Mama wanted English, so I have two names. Whichever you prefer is fine with me.

"You've lost your mother, and your da?

I should have said she was just back a bit but say, "She died. Da was transported, far away somewhere."

"It is a bad time when girls as young as you are alone."

I cannot take it back now. At least now, maybe if they are willing, I can look like I am part of their family.

Maebh comes right to me and quits crying. She snuggles into my arms. I smell her skin and thoughts of baby Bridie come despite my resolution. Her skin is sweet, and she is so birdlike. There are other smells not so sweet coming from her. Even those are better, homier, than the smells which surround us. I stop momentarily to rearrange her. She murmurs then falls into a deep sleep.

Suddenly Shamus looks back and says, "We have no food to share."

"I am not wanting, so ask none of you."

At that, Deirdre gives me a shy smile and says, "Sorry, it is just that now…"

"I understand, some may be kind just to get a bite to eat. I am fortunate, I have a bit of food." There is not much, and I try to make light of it. "At least I have a shift under this dress and if I have to, even my shoes can be bartered."

Deirdre shakes her head. "I thought someone would help—instead it has been horrible workhouses. Indian corn from America nearly killed us. We were all sick because we tried it. They even want us to pay for it in coin when the people here have always bartered for what we need, and those horrible make-work projects.

"My brother sold his only coat. It was the last thing he had. Then, desperate, he got a place working on a road, despite the freezing rains. They didn't even give him what he needed to get enough food much less a shelter! He and his are all gone now. Sorry, there I go again. Anyway, we don't have much, but we can be traveling companions. What is your destination?"

"I am on the road to my grandmother's house in Antrim County north of Belfast."

"We are going to Belfast with hopes of getting to America."

"I have heard that the best way is to take a boat to Liverpool and then to America."

"We heard the same. It is most likely the way we will go also. I dread the prospect of the journey in the bottom of the boat as ballast, but it may be our only option. I especially fear for her." She looks fondly at the girl asleep in my arms. "I hear it is the hardest on the littlest ones but what do we do? We all will likely starve or die of disease if we stay here."

I nod my head.

Thank heavens, this soggy day is nearly at an end. Shamus carries their two big quilts. They are soaked, but I help him spread them on the road. The ground would be nicer, but high, stone fences keep us out of the yards. Even though I fall off the quilt when I roll over as I sleep, I am warmer and feel safer than I would have on my own.

I sleep with my apron curled around me both for warmth and to protect my food from the hands of the wretched people who surround us. I dream of my warm pallet near the fire and all the potatoes I can eat.

I wake starving, but I allow myself only a few berries. I did not tell Deirdre about the coins in my shoes. The fair folk did not take them. I am grateful for their honesty. They could have so easily. I will have to use them for Indian corn or some other food. Maybe I can find herbs to sell. I lost all mine somewhere, but with all the fences I cannot even see the fields. I want to eat more. The wind freezes my bones, today. I am so hungry. I do not complain, I have so much more than many here.

More and more people push themselves onto this roadway. It would seem that with this many people there would be more noise but even the babies seem too drained to cry. The only sound is caws from greedy birds. I watch them tear apart a body in the road. Some men think to scare them away but the ravens peck at the intruders with their blood spattered white beaks. Their raucous chorus gives me shivers.

About midday a farmer joins the throng with his cart full of oats. I can smell them under the tarp. My stomach is not the only one growling. It probably is destined for the coast. There is a lot of muttering. A man who must have sold his clothes, since he only wears a ragged shirt says, "Irish soil grew this food, the Irish tenants tended it. There it goes for bellies in England, I wager."

Another, in nearly the same condition, warns, "I was nearby

when a bunch of men attacked a wagon. The wagoner had men with clubs. All anyone came away with were some bashed heads. I won't try. It is a shame to see food, justly ours, being carted off while we starve."

There are more complaints but most sink back into a horrible silence. The only sounds are ravens and shuffling feet.

I had hoped to talk more with Deirdre as we walked, but it is taking all my strength just to move my feet today. Maybe there will be a chance later.

I just wish the ravens would go away. They perch on the fences to watch us with their beady black eyes. I suppose they need food too, just not us, not now.

I have to make Maebh walk all of the time today. At least she is able to hold my hand more easily than her mother's who is taller than me. Maebh is crying again until her wee brother brings her a few yellow flowers.

She sticks them towards my face. "Smell. Pretty."

They do smell good.

She is paying all her attention to the flowers now, so sometimes she trips, and I have to keep her from falling. That is fine with me. I am as thrilled with the small gift as she is. Where did he find them?

They are bedraggled as we come to the end of the day. The next morning, she finds four stems and continues to carry them. There are only a few watery petals and the bright greens of yesterday are nearly brown. She no longer holds them up but refuses to let go of her pretties.

The ravens are the only ones who look well fed. Well, ravens and the drivers of the carts and their guards. At first the goons walked with the rest of us. Now they sit on top of the carts and stare around as if to dare us to give them a reason for them to take a swing. Is there anyone stupid enough to start something?

Just then, a shaggy man and his friends do try to undo the ropes of the canvas covering the load of grain. The whole stramash is done in seconds. Their bodies are shuffled to the side of the road unceremoniously.

The ravens leave their perches as if signaled. Their black bodies in flight remind me of a bride's black Chantilly lace veil from another life. Time seems to slow as their great procession whirls to the ground. Kisses not of love but craving, poke at lips and eyes... I look away. I cannot stop the sounds. The horrible chorus of caws as they fight over the body. This road, far more horrible than any place I have ever been, makes me want home. I want to wake from this nightmare. The flies and the smell of death almost drive me mad. I want to smell the ocean, even dead fish, anything but this. Just keep my mind on Grandmother. When I reach her, she will take care of me.

There are rumors daily of a soup kitchen but the ones who have looked for them come back even more hungry and exhausted. They tell us that there are only soupers, folks who want to trade food for our souls. A bowl costs a name on the rolls of the Protestants. The stories of the workhouses are enough to keep most of us on the road to the last.

"Tonight, we will be in the village of Lorgain." says Deidre

"I have to go into the village here, also. I ate the last of my food yesterday. The food here is much more expensive than when I started this trip with Mama." How would we get enough food if she and the boys had survived? I think about the coins but decide against in favor of selling my shift. Who knows what I may need the coins for someday?

She looks sadly at the quilts trailing down her husband's back. "We will sell the smaller of the quilts. We are all so thin now, we can fit on the big one. Such a pity. I thought I could hand it down to my children. My mother's mother made it. I used to trace the Celtic design with my finger when I was as little as Maebh is now. I was fascinated with the way it went over and under, never ending.

There is a crowd around the plump man in his dark wool vest and white shirt. He stands on a box in the center of the road. It nearly stops traffic, but he does not seem to mind. He leans down to give a small boy a stack of clothes. The pile is so large the boy staggers, recovers his balance, and then runs off with them. One shirt drags in the mud.

Deirdre joins the crowd next to a woman waving a skirt above her head. "Is this the one who buys cloth here? What does he trade? I do not see anything."

The woman looks annoyed but says, "He gives scraps of paper. You have to take them to the shop over there to trade for food."

We join the throng, holding the shift and quilt as high as we can so he will notice us.

He spots the quilt. "Now there is an ugly quilt. It should probably be thrown in a fire, but any cloth will do. Linen?"

Deidre looks hurt. "Yes. It is an heirloom and good quality. Filled with wool not seagrass."

He lifts it. "Well it is heavy enough I will give you a chit for it."

I am startled when Deirdre says "Three."

"I don't barter with beggars."

She pulls the quilt out of his hands. His bushy eyebrows lift with surprise, but he reaches for it again. "Two then."

I see the tears in Deirdre's eyes as she lets it go. He hands her the small sheets of paper and she is gone.

I have to wait for several others before he sees me.

He reaches for my shift. "One" he says.

"But look at the fine embroidery and the lace on the bottom." I plead.

Without taking a second glance he says, "One. Take it or get out of the way."

I take it.

I go to the shop where I find Deirdre getting her two chits worth of food. I am appalled at how little she gets.

I complain to her, "The man who bought my shift did not even look at the lace or the embroidery."

Deirdre snorted. "He wouldn't give you more for embroidery, they make paper from the clothing in England. Their books come off of our backs!"

Books are wonderful but what a sad price.

****

This road has seemed endless, one day, after the next, after the next. How much farther can it be to Belfast?

As we leave town, Deirdre says, "It is about time to give up and go to a workhouse. They have one here in Lorgain."

Seamus, her husband, hears her and roars. "I will hear none of it."

I was surprised that he had that much strength still.

We wrap the last quilt around all of us tonight. I am both glad I could sell my shift and heart-broken to see everyone around us stripped to only the barest of rags.

Misery has become like the fog which will no longer let me see more than where I am to take my next step. My mind is dull to the point I almost do not care to even take another. I put one foot in front of the other out of habit. The one bright spot which helps me get up in the mornings is the thought of my grandmother and how happy I will be to see her face. I imagine that she looks like an older version of Mama with the same violet eyes as Mama and I have, or maybe, hers are more like Aunt Annie's, green.

One step after another. As I hear the squish of each step, it is a reminder of how good it is my shoes are still on my feet. The roads have become so terrible with the slime of the sick. I slide and catch myself against a wall. I need to get back to the center. Just in time, I miss a man who cannot keep the Indian corn down.

We all have to use it for any of the common urges. It is so crowded we have little room to even avoid tripping over the person in front of us if they pause. I have a moment of hope when someone says that we will soon be in Belfast. Maybe there we will have more room.

"We will soon be parting ways," says Deirdre, "I do not think you should go to the docks with us."

"I thought I would stand on the dock and wave as you left," I tell her.

"Then you would be alone there. I do not think that is a place for a good girl as you have reminded us you are. Do not go to the docks unless you have a destination such as getting on one of the ships. The docks are dangerous places to wander around without anyone to watch out for you. Avoid them if possible."

"Worse than the roads have been?"

"Yes, far worse. Promise me, if you can avoid the docks, you will."

I nod assent. Deirdre has become a good friend and I trust her. I do not want to part ways, but it is almost time. We are coming into Belfast and I need to go north while she leaves to the west for Liverpool. There is a break in the clouds and the first blue sky I have seen in days. I would rather to have had time for long goodbyes, but the road is too crowded. The best I can do is give Maebh a quick hug and give a squeeze to Deirdre's hand with a quick "Thank you. God speed.

Chapter 11:
Falling into It

I watch as Maebh disappears down the street and say a small prayer for her safe passage. Then I go to the left. Hopefully, I can find the way to get to the road north out of Belfast, and there will be someone to buy my apron. Tied tightly, it keeps the hunger pains away. For the last several days there has been no food.

There are too many people, we look like bunches of sticks. An old woman trips and falls into me. Her boney shoulder hurts. I can hardly breathe because of the crowd. Who thought I could miss the time when we started on the road? There was always a yard or field near the edges—here, only buildings, people, and stench.

Up ahead, a man stands with his arms full of clothes. Finally, a cloth buyer. As I get close, he puts up his hands and says, "That is all for today. Come to this same place tomorrow." he winks dramatically, "If you are lucky, I will be buying here."

What faint hope! I have nothing left, but the coins in my shoes. I will not go to Grandmother's empty handed. I hope to at least find a family to stand around. This was my chance to get some food and leave tonight. It has been a long time since I felt so desperate. The sun is starting to sink behind a building. Darkness fills me.

There, the small walkway between the buildings is just big enough for me. I need a few minutes to be alone. Then I will try again. I do not want to be jostled by anyone.

My apron catches. I pull to get it away from whoever has me.

The snap of broken wood makes me realize it just caught. My heart does a jig for a while.

It is dark and cool here. There is a strange smell. I thought it would smell musty, or even have a stench like the streets do. This smells more like Mathair's cottage. I push back into the space as the last light vanishes. Startled again, as a rat or maybe a dog brushes by me in the darkness. I jump back into a wall. It releases with a crack. Suddenly, looking up from the floor, I see rafters covered with bundles of herbs in various stages of drying.

A groomed, grey head stares down at me. "Should I do away with you now or just throw you out into the street? What are you doing here anyway? You splintered my latch. Get on with you now." His piercing grey eyes glower at me in the faint light of a fire.

I struggle to my feet. "I am sorry. I did not mean to be here. The smells reminded me of a place where I lived." I fumble in my apron pocket and pull out crumbs of herbs and salts to show him.

I break out crying. Scared, the words tumble out. "I smelled your plants when I was trying to find a place to get away from all the people. I am sorry, I will leave. It is just—the wall opened, and I fell. My friends told me I could not find herbs anywhere around here. I sold herbs at Enniskillen after Mathair, not my real mother, Caitlin O'Neill, she found me. She taught me and…"

"Stop this blathering right now!"

He glares at me—then he smiles broadly. "You know Caitlin? Have not heard from her for years. Is she well? I thought I would travel to see her at least once more but with the troubles and getting slower, well…" He pulls at his beard.

"I am sorry. Her sister-in-law, we met by chance on the road, told me her name was Caitlin and that she is dead. She also gave me a small kettle as a gift, but I lost it on the way here. I am on my way to see my real grandmother who lives north of Belfast. I think it will only take me about three or four days to get to her house. I am out of food. I thought I would sell my apron and have enough but the man who was buying cloth just outside..."

"Stop! First, what is your name? Mine is O'Brian."

"My name is Mary or Máire depending on whether it was my mama or da speaking. I answer to either. Mrs. O'Neill called me her daughter's name, Ellen and made me call her Mathair."

"So, Caitlin taught you to identify herbs, did she? Are you any good?"

"I could have spent a lifetime learning more, but she praised me for learning well. She seemed to be able to remember everything about them but not what we had just eaten for breakfast. These are what remain."

"I see you have some salts also. How did you get those?"

"I found them in a cave near Enniskillen." I do not tell him about Kalen's help.

He eyes me with one brow raised but then goes on, "If you will go to where I tell you to get herbs, I think I can supply your needs for the rest of your trip." He says, fingers stroking his beard. "Some of the herbs I need for myself are not near here. Even with all I know about remedies, it gets harder every day for me to go out to collect herbs. There is no cure for getting old.

I will still go out during the day and make my rounds. I know...I know it is not done now, but it is how my da ran his business. Would you be my assistant? You could keep your apron."

This is an answer to my prayers. "Of course, I would love to help you. Do you have anything at all I can eat. I am very hungry. Where can I sleep? I will start first thing tomorrow."

"This parched corn is all I have on me now. You have to chew it for a long time before you swallow."

It is new to me and very hard. My teeth, sore already, hurt even more. I chew anyway. It fills my stomach.

I thought he might live among the herbs like Mathair did, but at last he gets up and looks around. "There is no bed here, but you can make a place to sleep under my workbench over there. I don't want to trip over you in the morning before I have enough light.

"Use whatever you find to make a pallet, I will bring some cloth and we can get some sweet grass tomorrow. I will also bring some porridge for you to eat in the morning, but you will have to wait until we finish with the herbs to eat it. We need to start first thing." He pats me on my head and then after pushing the bookshelf back to cover the way I entered, He disappears through a door I had not noticed.

****

He does not wake me. Light shines through a few cracks in the walls. Have I slept for a few hours or days? I don't know. He sits and reads by the light of an oil lamp. It is enough for me to see shelves to the ceiling.

Not wanting to disturb his studies, I walk up behind him as he reads. Beside his oil lamp is another book. I lean over to read the title. I bolt upright. "*Principia Mathematica!* Newton?" I gasp, and want to hold it, but stop my hands an inch from the cover.

The old man looks up in surprise.

"How is it you even know about this book and can read the title?

"My da held this book second only to the Bible! He declared it the second greatest book of all times! You have it!"

"Did he know Newton was English?"

"I don't know. He said the book was in Latin but not anything about Newton."

"I prefer Leibniz's treatment of the calculus better, but it does have much to recommend it. I am glad you are awake. I wanted you to gather some herbs before it got too late in the day. We will leave

85

through the front door. I have no intention of revealing my bolt hole by too much traffic."

"Mathair usually had us gather them before breakfast. Sorry, I meant Mrs. O'Neil. I will probably always think of her as Mathair. Anyway, yes, and thank you."

As we leave, I realize his place is in the back of a stable. It is well kept and has an earthy smell of hay and horse droppings. Horses stomp and neigh as we walk between the stalls. I scratch one of the black heads as we walk by.

It is early, the misty streets are almost empty except for people asleep near the walls. We head back on my route into the city until we are almost out of Belfast when we turn south.

"Watch where I take you carefully. I will not show you again."

"I wish you had told me earlier." I sigh.

"You are a smart girl. You will remember. The path gets more difficult to follow here."

We go out of the city completely and into what must be the back of a large estate. The newly harvested oat fields remind me of the grain carts which passed us on the road, filled with the grain to save us had they not been bound for England and other ports.

I bring myself back, sharply, and look to see where I am. It is too easy to think about those days and miss my way entirely when I come back alone next time.

"See the forest over there and the fields, those are the Lord's hunting grounds. While there are many herbs to be found there it is patrolled regularly. I almost got caught myself recently. My ears are not what they used to be. It is protected by a blackthorn hedge. I can show you how to get through but for now we stay only outside the hedgerows."

It is cool but nice walking through the country. Neither of us say anything for most of the time. I think about little Maebh and her family. Are they on the boat to Liverpool? I will never know.

Occasionally I spot an herb he has not seen.

His smile wrinkles his face. "You have sharp eyes, girl." Each time we discover a new herb he asks, "What is this called? How is it used? How long can it be stored?" Mathair has taught me well. I am glad to know her instructions were accurate on the herbs even though the rest of her memory was gone.

On the way back to his workshop he takes me to meet his sister.

"What are you doing with this drowned rat? Get this urchin and the vermin she carries out of here!"

He closes the door behind us. "I guess you will not be welcome there. She never has taken to strangers, but I did hope she would look at you more like a lost kitten than a rat. You can stay at the workshop. I do think the idea of getting you clean and more bug free is a good one."

Once back at the stables he gets a horse bucket and soap and scrubs me thoroughly on arms, legs, and hair. He starts to lift my dress, but I make a small squeak. He backs off and hands me a soapy rag and one with just water and turns around to look at the bookshelf.

"Now" he says, "there is a lot of work to be done. Some of the herbs must be decocted right away."

Mathair only dried herbs to store them so I watch carefully, getting bottles and stirring as required.

He continues, "My sister hates this smell. Always has. Our da did this in our cottage when we were young. When a friend told me, he thought this place might be available I decided to move my herbs over here. Strange in a city so overcrowded, I would have two places rather than one. The owner does not ask money from me, rather he just wants liniment for the horses and himself. I should be more grateful."

He looks wistful. "I had high hopes when I was young. I planned to be a scholar and leave this town forever. I had learned about herbs from Da, but thought I was too good for all of that.

"When I took the books, I thought they were all the companions I would need. I find I sorely miss the company of the scholars and the arguments which went on late into the night."

I nod. He needs no more encouragement to continue with his tale.

"I got the first of my books when the gentleman for whom I was a sizar,"

I interrupt. "What is a sizar?"

He sighs, "At Trinity College in Cambridge in England, a poor man, such as myself, who had enough basic education, could seek employment of sorts with a gentleman as a manservant. I got my room, board, and most of my tuition payed. I was lucky. Your Newton here, went to Cambridge, but was no more than a subsizar, kitchen help." He turns away and under his breath says, "Might have found another gentleman or turned subsizar. Ah, the foolishness of youth."

Looking me in the eye he continues. "Anyway, when my gentleman came home from a trip to Spain with the yellow fever, I was nearly frantic. He died despite all the doctors and I did. I thought I would never have another chance to have the books I adored.

"I did not take all of them. Just the Newton, Leibniz, and any books by women. I took the chance his parents did not know what he had. He had told me they did not care for women in philosophy. He laughed when he said they did not even know it was now called science. I took a bigger chance on the Newton and Leibniz, but I had to have them.

"They had always wanted their son to go into the clergy and would have just sold them, anyway. Who had enough money, I ask you? I knew the books were not mine, still I had loved them. I grabbed those few volumes and came home to Belfast to be the herbalist my da had wanted me to be. I have always been afraid they would find out and set the authorities on me. I couldn't stay at Trinity because they would have had me thrown in prison for stealing."

I stand open mouthed. Why would he tell me all this?

He gathers many herbs and puts them into a large basket. After he carefully wraps some bottles and arranges them just so, he looks at me. Then he turns on his heel and heads for the door. "Thank you for your help and company. I will see you here early tomorrow." He leaves quickly.

The porridge he brought me before dawn is good even though cold. So is the silence. The thought of going outside now with all the people makes me shiver. The only sounds in here are the horses and the coos of doves. They bring my attention to some small windows high on the walls. I pull over a stool, so I can open the shutters for more light.

There are more books here than I have ever seen. I have only seen the one, the Bible, which was in Latin. Da did not have any in the Gaelic or English. Mr. O'Brian left three books on the table by his chair. I do not think he would mind if I sit and look at them for a while.

The brown leather of the *Principia* is both rich and inviting, and I love the little gold plants on the edges of the covers. I think giving our clothes to make books like this almost might be fitting. Then I think of the shivering and still starving people on the road. No, it is not.

Even though I can read Latin, the words inside do not make much sense to me. There are drawings, but they are only lines and circles and a fold out page with what looks like a comet.

Da drew a picture of a comet for his students. It seems long ago now.

Some of the other books look interesting. There is one called

Opticks by Newton, but it is in English. The pictures drawn in the margins seem to be something about light. There is another brown book in English by Mary Somerville. I want to learn how to read more English. She has my name. I wish I could understand it. Maybe the old herbalist could help me read her book. There is a word in the title, "s-c-i-e-n-c-e". I believe it is the word Mr. O'Brian used to describe the books he took.

The one at the bottom of the pile is the most beautiful book I have ever seen. It looks fun and exciting. The back is white leather. The cover is swirls of reds, yellows, and blues. Inside, there are pictures of people and birds, not just lines and circles. This is the most wonderful book ever! It is not Latin but close enough, I can get the meaning of a few words. Emilie du Châtelet wrote it, another woman. At the back there are drawings of lines and circles like drawn in the Newton's *Principia*. Did she study the same things he did?

I could stay here forever. Would Mr. O'Brian teach me what is in these books and feed me? He needs someone to go and pick and help prepare the herbs for use. It would help him and not be charity.

Wandering over to the table—no, he calls it a bench, there are all sorts of things. One of them is a glass square cut from one corner to the other so the ends look like triangles. There was a drawing of this in Newton's book, *Opticks*.

Scrabbling onto the bench where the light from the window shines, I hold the piece of glass, so the light goes through it. It works like the picture in Newton's book. On the opposite wall is a little rainbow. At first it is rather pale. I shut the other shutter to darken the room. Now, it is light and beautiful like the fair folk's cloth. Do they know about this glass trick? I wish I could show Kalen.

Chapter 12:
Could This Be Home?

Day 1. This is my new journal. O'Brian hates my handwriting but insists I write in here every day. He claims he will teach me to have a beautiful hand like he does. His is beautiful, not even Da's writing was as elegant as his! He makes me practice using a stick on the floor. My hand gets tired and my writing is never what he wants. Secretly, I like my writing. O'Brian says, "It looks like a little girl's."

I told him "I am a little girl."

He snorts at me, "You keep growing like you have been, and you won't be for long."

I like my life here. We have a routine. He comes in earlier than I wake most days and reads until I am ready to go.

The birds chirping in the rafters wake me. He does not let me eat right away. We must do our work first. After we get back, we take care of what we gathered. Then I stay here all day alone while he makes his rounds. I get to eat my porridge as soon as he leaves. He comes back in the evening. Normally, he is in a fine mood having sold the herbs and spent the day chatting with customers.

We spend the first part of each evening reviewing the lessons from the night before. I don't like that much. He expects a lot of me.

I can read and write some English now.

We use Mary Somerville's book. When we started, I begged him. "Please, let me learn from Emilie du Châtelet's beautiful book or even Newton's with the gold edges."

O'Brian just looks at me like he thinks I am daft. "What are you thinking, girl. Neither one of those is in English."

"Why can't I learn French first? I already know Latin. Why not use it?"

He sighs. "Think about where you live. English is the language here. You can agree to learn it or find someone else to teach you."

I still wish it was the pretty du Châtelet book. When I do really well, he lets me hold it and look at the pictures. When he first told me he might let me look at it, my work was never good enough. Today I got to look at it for just the second time.

He wants me to write with an elegant hand and gets frustrated with my slow progress. When we start our discussions, we both forget our irritation . Sometimes we even do small experiments.

****

I have wanted to ask him to let me go with him during the day, tonight I will do it. Before he has a chance to say anything I ask, "Could I go on your rounds with you tomorrow? I am sure I could help somehow."

"No! First, you have no genteel looking clothes to wear. At one time I did have common folk for customers. They still need herbs but seldom have anything to trade as the price for food is so high. They would not think anything of how you dress. Now, I have to keep up my appearances. Second, my customers know I am a bachelor and would think it not proper to be with a girl, nor do you have proper manners. Correctness is everything to some of them."

Why would being a girl matter to his customers? I do not steal,

I have always paid for my own way.

He breaks into my thoughts. "You do need some new clothes. Maybe I can trade for them. You have gotten tall. Your dress is almost indecent. I will see what I can do. You still can't come with me. Maybe later, if we work on your pronunciation and manners. Hmm. It might help.

"I will start teaching you to speak like you are from Cambridge. I could make up a story about an orphaned child, maybe a second cousin. It will take a while, but I think it might work if you have some patience."

I am sorry I cannot go with him. I don't like to be out with so many strangers now, but I do want to go out and see the city. I go to Mass on Sunday. I thought I might see O'Brian but perhaps he goes somewhere else. It is a large city.

****

Now, I wish I had not suggested he take me with him. He corrects every word I say. I do not speak at all because I am frustrated. I did not know he could switch back and forth from Irish, English with an Irish accent, and this formal English.

As we walk along looking for herbs, he starts telling me of his past. "I went to Cambridge you know. It took a lot of work to even get enough for the basics. Ship's passage was not cheap like it is now. I had to buy my own clothes and food. If I had only known Trinity College in Dublin had sizars. It would have been so much more affordable to go to Dublin, I would have started earlier.

"My uncle was educated and taught me. Without his tutoring, I would not have gone anywhere. Even with his lessons, I wasn't sure I would get into the university when I left for England."

We stop to pick some dandelions. He gives me some and tells me to eat them. They are especially bitter.

93

"These are terrible." I tell him.

"Don't talk back, girl. Notice how your gums don't bleed and you feel better since I started making you eat these herbs? Eat some of the rose hips, too. They will help the body in general and keep your teeth in your head."

We walk in silence some more, my shoes wet from the dew. The mist is lifting, and the sparks of light remind me of the hall of the *aos sí*. The sky is so blue, everything else lush and green.

O'Brian stares across the field. "Back then I sounded like I had been speaking the Gaelic all my life and had just learned English. Being from Belfast, it was a wonder I even spoke the Gaelic."

I am delighted by the turn in the conversation.

"My grandmother insisted. It still helped back then. Some of my father's customers were old or rural enough it is all they spoke.

"Anyway, I was lucky. I met my young gentleman the day I got to Trinity in Cambridge. He had recently inherited a great sum and wanted to look the part. He insisted that I speak properly. I felt like an octopus took up residence in my mouth when I started. You'll get the hang of it. At least you speak English. So many from the west do not."

"I hope I can."

"I will not push you any more today. I forget how hard it was at first. So how is your reading coming? You haven't read for me in over a week. I need to teach you some more of the maths, too.

"Also, I have an idea from further along than you have read in Mary Somerville's book. I want to discuss it with you."

He bends down to pick some nettles. I am glad his attention to the way I talk is broken.

He continues. "You know we have been having trouble getting our tinctures just right. In her book Somerville talks about light, how the length of the wave is different for each color. I had the idea there must be some way to use this, so we can stop the procedure at just the right place by cooling the mixture when it is perfect. I want you to look in *Opticks* to see if Newton has anything which might give a clue on how to make our machine. This will be fun. It is almost like being among the scholars again."

It is later than usual when we get back to the stable, I shake like a dog to get the moisture out of my hair. I use the comb O'Brian gave me to get the rat's nests out of it. Padraig's hair was the worst for matting. It has been a long time since I thought about my brother. God, please let your light shine on all of my family, including Da. I hope he is doing well in his new land.

Day 137. O'Brian wants me to change how I talk as well as how I write. He says he is very pleased with the progress of my handwriting. I do like how it looks now. I was thinking of my family today. I hope they are all safely in heaven, except for Da of course. I hope I will meet them there someday. I am going to mass on Sunday even though it gets harder to push through the people on the streets.

O'Brian has said he will get me some new clothes. My only dress has become too short and has many holes. I fix them as well as I can. He has a needle that he uses for a compass in a bowl of water. He lets me use it to sew my clothes, but it is almost a lost cause.

We are attempting to make a machine to measure the color of his tinctures. I am supposed to research the books we have here. I wish there were more. I recently learned there is a library in

Belfast, The Linen Hall Library. O'Brian would dearly love to have enough money to have a subscription to it, but it is much too costly. I would like to just peek inside. I never thought I would be such a bookworm. He brings the books to life.

O'Brian slams the door so hard the whole room is shaking. I don't say anything.

"Malthus! Damn Malthus!"

Is it an herb or a person?

He drops his Cambridge accent and talks in an Irish brogue. It sounds so much like Mama's, tears come to my eyes.

"Sorry, it is not you. A customer, I doubt she even remembers I'm Irish, started spouting how right it is the peasants are dying.

She said, "Everyone knows Malthus, a cleric of the Church of England, who wrote it is a positive thing for the poor to have famines and epidemics so the numbers will match the food supply."

"Malthus indeed used the word positive, but I think he meant 'certain', not 'good'. I happen to know her husband has made his fortune in making whiskey from Irish grain to supply the English! It was all I could do to stay civil long enough to leave without destroying a long-term relationship. I cannot afford to lose her as a customer."

I stare at him blankly.

"You don't know who Malthus is? Oh, of course not. He's been dead for a while, but he wrote a book. He said the population, the number of people, would naturally at some point exceed the food available. It is indeed a part of what happened but not all of it. Much of the suffering comes from the lousy government the English have given us.

You remember you told me about how your family was evicted and they even tore your cottage to the ground? Do you know why?"

I wipe my eyes on my sleeve. "No. Not really."

"When the potatoes started rotting, someone in England had an idea. They would tax the Irish landlords to pay for the relief and charge them so if the tenants wanted to emigrate, the landlords would have to pay. The taxes were not based according to how much land they owned, but on the number of tenants who were on their land. Many landlords had never been to Ireland. They relied on overseers. When the count came back, they were shocked. They had a choice to pay a lot in taxes or..."

"Or throw us out of our houses." My eyes fill with tears again when I think money was so important to them, they would let a sweet baby like Bridie die in the cold.

"Some of the landlords felt like they had to do that or lose their land. A fate most considered worse than death, their own, not the tenants."

"Worse than having Da transported and my whole family dying?"

"No. I agree with you. What has been done is intolerable."

"Da said the English have hated and hunted us for years. They just want the Irish dead or gone."

"Some, yes, but did you know many people of the Church of England including Queen Victoria have collected money to send to the starving here?"

"I don't understand."

"The government was run by the Tory party when the famine started. When the Whig party took over, they put Trevelyan in charge of the relief. He was influenced by people who championed Malthus and the idea of *laissez-faire* or hands off, which means the interest of business should be first no matter what. In truth, it was like he had declared war, and probably kills as many as the black potatoes.

I look at O'Brian with horror.

"You have traveled through some of the worst. Not everyone, especially around here, were as afflicted. You can understand why I am so frustrated.

"I think the lady only thinks of it as a way to justify the fact so many are dying. It is a popular idea in England now, even though not all English agree."

I sit in shock. I have nothing to say. It had all been so simple to understand before. Now it will take some time to think about all he has said.

Chapter 13:
So Much Hope

"What have you found for me in your studies on light, Mary? Have you found anything you think will help us measure color?" O'Brian says as he takes off his coat on returning from his rounds. I wish he would at least greet me.

I reply, "Newton and Mary Somerville use some words that could be Greek. Every time I think I have figured it out in English they say something which should be plain, but it is so hard I want to throw the book in the fire."

"You are doing well. It will be worth the time if we can get it to work. Go on with it, I have watched you. I am sure you have something."

I smile. "I did find something in Mary Summerville's book. When two light sources are the exact same wavelength the brightness doubles."

"Too imprecise." He starts.

"Come outside. I think I can show you." I have a pan of water. "See the sun is directly overhead. We are lucky today. It is not covered with clouds. Watch the light on the bottom of the pan when I use this stick to disturb the water from both sides at once. See how some places it makes bright lines on the bottom. Those lights are made where the light doubles because of being the same wavelength."

O'Brian scratches his beard like he is not certain. but I can tell from his eyes, he is excited.

I continue. "We could use mirrors to make certain our original light for two vials of solution is the same so the brightness doubles as we expected, and what it looks like when it does. The final light should be twice as bright as our original light. Then we replace one vial with the same color by turning a prism so only a small portion of the spectrum shines through a slit. At some point we see the brightness of the combined lights double. Here is the best part! See this in Mary Summerfield's book.

He reads it. Then nods when he is done. "Do you think we might turn it, so it is a half-wavelength coming through the slit? Rather than doubling, the combination would go black. I think it would be the exact time to take our solution off the fire."

He stands then, staring at the ceiling blankly, silently for a long time, then adds, "It might work. The biggest problem I see with it, is we need bright light. If we lived in Spain where it is sunny, we could use sunlight. This is Belfast. We can't trust the light from the sun will be bright enough when we most need it."

"You are right. It is a problem. Do you have any ideas?"

"I have one. I think your idea has enough merit. I'll work on it."

I smile as I add, "The other problem was the glass. We need both prisms and mirrors to make this work. Luckily I found something on my way to gather herbs yesterday I think will suit the bill perfectly." I pull out the large basket, usually reserved for my best herbs, and with a flourish remove the cloth covering it. There is a thick glass mirror, broken but not shattered with beveled edges so it can be ground into perfect prisms. His jaw drops.

"I found it in a ditch, and I wanted to show you immediately, but then I decided to wait until after we discussed my idea." I am so excited. I know I look like a little girl as I bounce up and down. "Perfection?"

"Wonderful. I have a surprise for you also." He pulls a bundle tied with string out of his bag. It is a blue material. When I finally get it untied, it is a dress.

Without taking off my old dress, I slip the new one over my head. I swirl my skirts around. I am so pleased with it even though it is large on me. The waist has to be tied tightly with the sash to look right, but I don't care.

O'Brian gives me a gruff look. "In all my days I never thought I would be buying a dress for a girl. I am glad the cloth buyer would let me look through his wears. It only cost two arms and a leg."

I smile. "Would it crack your face like an egg to do more than frown? Thank you again." I almost fall from spinning so much.

"Watch yourself, girl! You will break something. By the way, I am going to take you out on my rounds tomorrow. Mrs. White is an old woman and a bit deaf. I have been preparing her, so she is looking forward to meeting my niece. I hope your new accent is sufficient. I don't think she would take kindly to you if she thinks you are Irish. It will be a good first test. At the other places you can stand outside and wait for me to return.

****

At our knock, Mrs. White's butler opens the door. He shows us into the parlor. I have never been in a place so grand. Yesterday I felt so elegant in my new dress but in this place, it feels like it should have remained a rag. Mr. O'Brian seems at home in such fancy surroundings, but I would rather be on the street.

Mrs. White's look seems suspicious when he introduces me as his niece.

I reply by curtseying, then say, "It is nice to make your acquaintance." I realize I do not know her title or if she has one. I feel my face get hot.

"My lady." O'Brian adds hastily.

"Please have a seat." She says, but her eyes say, look at what the cat drug in. "I have been looking forward to your visit Mr. O'Brian. The doctor has said he cannot help my rheumatism, so I have been hoping you might have something for me as well as the usual herbs and a nice visit." She glares at me briefly.

"Why yes, your ladyship. I have all the usual nostrums, and I will also give you this. I prepared it especially for you. Have your cook make a tea of it and drink it twice a day in the morning before breakfast and in the evening before bed."

Other than the introductions she ignores me for the rest of the conversation. I have the impression she prefers to talk to O'Brian alone. I wonder if many of his customers are women who care as much for his conversation as his herbs.

The day is long and boring. I hate being out on the street, while O'Brian chats with customers. Why did I think this would be a good idea? I practice my English accent with delivery people.

"Fine day don't you think?" I remark to a young woman delivering eggs.

She gives me a look but says nothing. I think I may have fooled her.

By the time O'Brian gets back, all I want to do is leave here quickly. He starts towards the stable but then turns.

"I thought we were going back and start our experiments." I say, trying to keep a whine out of my voice.

He hurries me in the wrong direction. "I have found a man who says he has a limelight. It was supposed to go into a theater but the place folded before it got started. It will solve our problem of the inconsistent light. This light is bright white, nearly blinding, but we can shutter it, so we have what we need and no more."

"Oh." I say. "That sounds perfect!"

"It is a little touchy. The problem is the fire can get out of hand. The hydrogen and oxygen are controlled by water cylinders. The man said, 'more than one man has regretted letting the darn things go dry.' He explained when the water evaporates, the flame works its way back to the source of the gasses and everything explodes.

We will have to be extra careful to watch it. When mixed properly the hydrogen and oxygen will make a flame against a piece of limestone. He said the positioning of the rock is a bit tricky, too. This will, however, give us a light we can use any time we need it. Just think! We are so close to being able to measure the color and perfect our process. Science will work for us yet."

After he leaves, I sit down to work on my diary. I have begun to enjoy it.

Day 162, I hope I can stay here forever. My grandmother may not even know I exist. She has never met me. I cannot imagine it could be better to live with her than to be here with O'Brian learning and doing science.

He does not seem to want me to leave. Everything is finally coming together. I have my new dress. O'Brian will soon have his machine for measuring color. We are ready for the last step, combining the light from the prism and the new tincture. It is so exciting. The new limelight has been perfect. We almost let the water dry once the other day, but I caught it in time. I need to be very careful.

"Get me the flask off the burner. Quickly. I think this is it. There. Put the new sample where the other one was. Careful." O'Brian is so excited he can hardly contain himself. "I've almost got it. Oh hell! The limestone needs to be adjusted. Just a minute. I…"

Whoosh.

Oh no! We forgot the water.

"O'Brian!" I scream.

103

His face and one hand are on fire. I throw a bucket of water at him, but he is already badly burned. I grab a tincture for burns and pour it on his hand and face. The smells are terrible, burnt hair, skin, tincture combine so I think I might get sick. I have to control myself. He needs me. I cover him more with my old dress. Should I wrap his head? All I have left is my bedding and it is full of germs. I wish Mathair was here to help me.

At least the fire did not spread. This whole stable could have gone up in flames. I need to get help. Where? His sister!

I run. Find his house, and pound on the door. She answers. I grab her hand and shove her shawl at her. We are out the door before I can tell her anything. As we walk quickly, I say, "It is O'Brian. An experiment went wrong. Hurry. He is burned."

She runs now with surprising speed. By the time we get back, the stable lads have smelled the smoke and found him. The doctor they must have called, arrives just after we do.

"We do not need you." his sister states.

"But this man is badly burned. I am a doctor, I must look at him," says the man carrying a bag. He continues to push his way past her.

She grabs his shoulder and shouts. "I have seen you bleeding patients. Get out of here. He does not need less blood!"

She gets his arm and spins the sputtering man out of the room. "Get my brother some of the horse blankets. Keep him warm." She carefully inspects the burns. "You have done well to get the tincture on so quickly. Now, where is the comfrey salve? Do we have anything that will work for bandages?"

I shake my head.

"No?" She starts tearing strips of her petticoat.

"We have to boil them." I yell. My desperation must show in my eyes because she stops and hands me the strips.

"Go ahead girl. He told me about your germs. Just hurry. Let them start to cool then hand them to me, one at a time. Get some tongs over there."

She does not even leave openings for his eyes. There are only small holes in the bindings for his nose and mouth. Done, her shoulders slump. "This place reeks," she says as she drops into the chair. "I always hated these smells. Is there any laudanum?"

I take it out of the hiding place. We keep it hidden because we have to pay for it. Why is the one thing that will help his pain the one we will have to have cash to get? If only we could grow it here.

I carefully drip it into his mouth. He gags but keeps it down. "...28, 29, 30. I am so glad he taught me about dispensing this by drops. Too much could kill him, you know. Can he survive the burns?"

"He is past the immediate danger, but we will have to wait. I would not have been able to care for him without your help," she says smiling at me. Maybe she will be my friend, now.

****

Each day we change dressings, give him more laudanum, and pray. The drugs are strong, but they do not relieve all the pain.

We can tell when he is sleeping because he is restless and moans. When he wakes, he is often scratching himself, from the effects of the laudanum. Each day we spend less of our money on food and more on the opium's black magic. He needs more it seems to get past the pain. He wails, thin and high, when we have none to give him. It is more than we can stand.

His sister has moved into the stable with me. The owner allows us to live here rent free. He also helped her to sell their house. The money is disappearing much too quickly.

He sleeps soundly for the first time in months. He has been in such pain. The scars on his face have finally turned from the angry red blotches to white spiderwebs. The stench is gone. We tie a cloth over his eyes to substitute for eyelids now after the rest of the bandages are gone. He is blind but any light seems to bother him.

His sister sits across from me. She is looking at the few coins we have.

I wish I could do more. "I am sorry I was not able to take his place in selling herbs. The ladies who used to demand herbs from him won't even let me in their doors. I wear my good dress and I am told my English would be acceptable to the most discriminating."

"Silly girl. You could never do what they want. They can get the herbs anywhere and cheaper. They want to be pampered and wooed. They want to be loved by a dapper man, more than they want his herbs. He will not be able to get those customers again. We could try to get back some buyers among the poor, but how can they choose between herbs and food."

"Yes, I have been meaning to talk with you about that. Not buyers, about the money. I know it is almost gone. I am as thin as when I first came into Belfast and you are a ghost of yourself compared to when I met you." Tears form even though I promised myself I would not cry. I blink them back. "I need to go find my grandmother. I should have left days ago but…"

Her blue eyes blurred with the white of age water also. "I have not said anything for days because I will miss you so much when you are gone. I am so sorry we did not get to know each other when you first came. No time for regrets." She brushes her tears away with a flick of her hand. "I can give you…"

"Not a thing! I will be fine." My voice is too loud, and I wake him.

"Wha? Wha…?" O'Brian shakes off the covers and sits upright.

"It is time for our girl to be leaving."

"No." His voice is the whimper of a child. "She can't leave."

"She must, sweet brother. I will be here for you. She needs her family."

"We are her 'amily."

"No. Let her go."

O'Brian, no longer able to shed tears, sobs with great heaves.

I squeeze his hand for the last time, grab my few things, and run into the road. In the soft rain, the smells of moss, the sea and death engulf me. Will I ever find a place that is truly home? I pray that grandmother, even though I have never met her, will take me in. If only Mama…

Chapter 14:
Violet Eyes

Glendunn at last. Almost to Grandmother's. I wish I had my diary and think of what I would say. Why did I forget it?

"Watch where you're going there, girl."

So caught up in my own thoughts, I run into a man wearing a suit with tails and a Derby hat. He stops and stares at me. I do the same. It seems like a moment of recognition, but I know I've never seen him. It's his violet eyes. Clouds at late sunset, Da said of Mama's. I have her violet eyes, and so does this old man in front of me. We both step back.

"I am sorry for running into you, Sir."

Something about him makes me doubt he ever apologizes to anyone. He turns quickly and walks down the road without a word.

An old woman, wearing a ragged shawl, who has seen this says, "If you know what is good for you—bettered not cross his path again."

I nod and turn to leave, but she goes on with her admonitions, "He is overseer for the lord of the estate near here. Many is the lass who has regretted his attention." Then the sound of footsteps and the clang of the gate let me know she has left.

I do not need a second warning. Shaken, I lean up against a wall for a few minutes.

Oh, no. I have missed my first chance to ask about my grandmother and where she might live. Straighten up, it is time to find the answer to my question.

This is a tiny town, there is only the one large building, probably the market, and the few cottages which line the road. The large building might be the best place to start. My feet reluctantly start up the path. Why hesitate now? This is the end of my very long journey.

If she is here, if she is still alive, will she like me? Can she feed me? I am almost out of the food I got in Belfast. I am so hungry, more than I was before I met O'Brian, if that is possible. I have to find her. Will she want me as a granddaughter as much as I want her for a grandmother?

Taking a deep breath, I open the door to the market. The door is not barred, but there are no people here. It's not right. There are always people in the market houses. I turn to leave when a black-haired, dark-eyed boy steps out of the shadows. "Father Flannery's funeral is at the end of town in the church on the right."

"What? Who is Father Flannery? Why?" I trail off, sputtering.

"I'm sorry. Let me start over. It's just you are not from here. They told me to tell any strangers where the funeral was, and I just thought..."

"I don't even know Father Flannery. I am Mary. This is the town nearest my grandmother's house, at least Mama said this is where we were headed." I sigh. "If I Mama were still with me, I would..."

"Are you an orphan? I am, too. Well I was. Eric and Clohe adopted me. I was in the workhouse. My name is Liam. They left me here today because I didn't know Father Flannery, either. They would have closed if I hadn't been here."

Surprised, I stare at him, as young as my Padraig and minding this place. "You were in a workhouse? I have heard so many stories. Is it as bad as they say?"

"My parents both died there. It was beyond description. We

only had a tiny space to sleep, we took turns. There was never enough to eat. So many got sick, they had their own graveyard.

"I have only been here a few months. Eric told me they want to keep me here as their own son. Still, they show a lot of trust in leaving me here."

"I am an orphan, too, or at least I think I am. My mama died on the way here. We think Da got transported.'

"So, you think there is a chance he is still alive?"

"I do, but Mama said we were to think of him as being dead. She was probably right. I still have trouble doing it. I prefer to think of him with a peg leg on a ship or maybe in Australia, tending sheep at night." I gaze across the room thinking of all those people, not just my family but the people I knew in County Clare. I shake my head to let them go again.

Here, I have the chance to ask about my grandmother and I almost forget a second time. "Do you know…?" Her name, what is her name? I have always called her Grandmother and I cannot remember her name! I know I heard it once when Bridie was born. Da was yelling that he would never name a child of his after…What is it? Oh, God, I have come so far to find her, please, just let me remember her name.

Finally, I share my problem with him, "I have come here from County Clare to find my grandmother and I don't remember her name. I know this is where she lived. I don't know if she is still alive. Anyway, Mama said she lived somewhere near your town. I…" With that, my feet will no longer hold me, and I find myself on the floor holding my stomach to fight off the hunger pains.

He quickly brings me a chair and helps me off the floor. Then he gets an old tin cup with water and hands it to me. He gives me a piece of fresh soda bread. I devour it.

"I can't eat fresh bread, no matter how hungry I get. Clohe makes it for me, and I hide it." He confides. "Da and Mum smelled like fresh bread when we got to the workhouse, but it was the odor of the typhoid. I got typhoid too, but I survived it, the only one of my family. There were six of us.

"My mum begged Da not to take us to the workhouse. He practically dragged her there. We were starving only Da and Mum were sick. None of the rest of us were at first. They took our clothes and gave us uniforms. They had spots and smelled like they hadn't been washed."

"The germs!" I say under my breath.

"I'll say there were charms, death wishes more like it."

I don't correct him just drink the water in silence. What will I do from here? What if I can't find her? Workhouses are worse than I had heard.

"The only way I saw my family was when I got sick. They separated us—the girls and boys in their own dorms, Mum in another and Da in a different one still."

Even though I am horrified at his story, I go to sleep sitting there. The cup falls.

Liam picks it up. He says, "We have a small shed behind the market. You can sleep there. It is empty right now. Maybe in the morning your mind will be fresh, and you can remember your grandmother's name. You're exhausted." He shrugs, "It's the best I can do. Probably, I wouldn't know her if you had a name. Sorry. But Eric and Clohe should."

He takes my hand gently, then helps me up like I am a great lady instead of a homeless orphan. He leads me outside.

Sunset. I think of the sunsets over the ocean. I look into the yellow, pink and finally violet sky. I am so close, maybe I will find her tomorrow.

He opens the door to the tiny shed and says "I won't lock it from the outside. There is a piece of wood you can use to bar the door.

The dirt floor is swept, and it looks clean. There is no window so when I do shut the door, there will only be the light that comes in around it. That is fine with me. No strangers.

"Goodnight, may God hold you in his hand until morning light."

"Goodnight, to you also. Thank you so much for this. It is a fine place, and I will feel much safer here than out by the road."

It really is the best place to sleep I've had since the stable in Belfast. I put my few things to one side. I do not even eat a single bite of my food. I cannot be guaranteed of finding her. I can't take chances now. Hopefully, tomorrow, it will all change, and I will be in my new home with my very own grandmother.

It must be dark outside now. Not even a hint of light comes through the shut door. I remember as a little girl, being so scared when it was very dark. Now it seems friendly and reassuring, I am safe for the night. I say my rosary and prayers for my family then drift off to sleep.

There is a booming sound in my dream. The storm is raging, and I cannot get my bearings. I wake to realize it is not a storm but the door. There is daylight around the edges of it. Someone on the other side is very insistent. I raise the bar.

A scarlet faced man holds his fist in the air, ready to hit the door again. He rears back as he sees me. I assume that this is Eric, Liam's new father.

He yells at me, "You little vagrant, what do you think you are doing here. Get out of this shed right now."

I quickly wipe my eyes of sleep. I can feel tears forming in them.

Fortunately, Liam, appears and pulls on the man's shirt. Almost faster than I can understand with his Ulster accent he says "I told her to sleep here. If I was wrong, I am sorry, but you were gone, and she was trying to find her grandmother but she couldn't remember the name and then her legs fell out from under her and I didn't know what…"

"Slow down boy." Eric's face goes back to a more natural color. He looks at me and says "So you are trying to find your grandmother. You think she is from around here." He finally takes a good look at me, pulling me farther outside so that he can see me better.

He asks, "Have you remembered her name yet?"

"Yes." My answer surprises me. I do remember. "Her name is Jenny Lynn McBride. Do you know her? Is she from around here?"

"Yes, I know her well and her whole family. Who did you say your mother is?"

"Was. She died of the fever when we were on our way here."

"I am most sorry to hear of your loss."

"Katie Lynn McCarthy."

His eyes close as he bows his head for a moment, then looks up and blows his nose. "Yes, I did know her. Did you know that she was the most beautiful girl in the county?"

I shook my head.

"Your da was the fiddler, wasn't he? I always thought that she fell in love with his fiddle. She loved to dance, you know."

I don't know what to say and so just stand there, silent.

"You have her violet eyes but not her hair. She was so fair."

I nod. Strange to have this man I do not know talk about my mother like he knew her well. Did he love her? It bothers me when he talks about her this way.

"Maybe I should have pursued her, more's the pity. Da told me to leave her alone. He said that there was trouble there but did not explain it. He was dead set against her. I was set to take over his market here and he threatened to turn me out. So, I courted Clohe instead and we have had a fine marriage."

I can feel my ears getting hot from embarrassment.

He finally seems to notice my discomfort and says, "Yes, I know your grandmother's place, but it is a ways out of town. She will be doing her marketing tomorrow most likely. You stay and she will come to you!" He sounds so pleased with himself.

I want to say no. I could find her myself if he would just tell me the way. I look down. I do not want to offend him. I would rather go right now.

"You should get cleaned up a bit before you meet her."

I look at myself. What a mess. No wonder he was a bit shocked to see me in his nice clean shed. I put my hand to my hair and find that it has bits of straw and even some mud. He is right, I need to get cleaned up and presentable for my first meeting with my grandmother.

He takes me out into the yard with a basin of water and a bar of soap. It smells like mint, the lather is pure heaven. He takes a pitcher of water and pours it through my hair to remove the suds. I take a cloth and a small towel into the shed to finish those parts that I am not willing to share with strangers.

A woman, Clohe probably, stands outside the door and says, "Hand me those filthy rags you are wearing and put this on." My blue dress should probably be burned but washing will have to do. Hers are much too big for me, so I tie the belt tight. They'll do. Honestly my clothes are a little big for me too. When I got them, they were already a little loose, but I have been losing weight since O'Brian got burned, they hang on me now.

Done, I go back into the warmth of the sun. The day is so bright I squint. The comb catches in my hair. It will take much of the day to get all the rats' nests out, so I am glad Clohe is in no hurry. When I am done, I feel little itches all over my body from bug bites. I don't know why I did not notice them when I was dirty.

"Come see, girl." She takes my hand and leads me into the building to a mirror. I almost do not recognize myself. I have bony arms and legs like when I first arrived in Belfast. My hair is dull and straggly. If I cut it, I could pass for a boy, but no not now. What will grandmother think of me? What if she doesn't believe me? What if she thinks I am just some urchin off the street? I won't go to the workhouse. I'd rather starve.

Chapter 15:
Almost There

My legs ache. The wait is agony. I should be glad they let me stay last night and now half the morning, but I want to go. My hair is combed, I am washed from stem to stern and so are my clothes. Clohe insists. They seem nervous, cleaning like they expect royalty. Any woman who comes to the door might be her.

"You'll scare away business. Get over here. We'll tell you when she comes." Clohe says.

"Is there anything about me that she will recognize?" With reluctance, I abandon my post by the door.

The man with the violet eyes stalks into the market. I look away before he sees me with a sigh of relief. He would have run into me a minute before. What is it, the stare he gave at first or maybe it was the warning from the old woman? I feel like snails are roaming my stomach, both hard and slimy.

"Humph, you never have anything!" He says, then slams the door.

I breathe again. I don't want to live so near to him. No choice.

I have to go outside. I need air but I peek out of the door first. No sign of him. Near the corner of the building there is a group of men and boys. Except for occasional glances at me, which I am sure they give any stranger, they talk and laugh.

One man pulls out a penny whistle and plays Sheebeg Sheemore which quiets the others. The haunting melody is one of my favorites.

When he starts on the Mo Mhaîre, tears form. Da used to play it on his fiddle to make me smile. This is not the time for crying. I walk down the road so no one will see me.

It feels good to stretch my legs. I have been walking for so many days. I got stiff standing so long. The mist cools my face and washes away the old pain.

It has taken so long to get here and now it will be today. Today, I will meet the family that I have never known. Today, I will have a home again with people who will love and care for me. Today, I can be a child. No, I've seen too much.

At the edge of the village, I turn around and go back. I start skipping. I have not skipped since home, but I feel like my heart may burst if I don't let some of this joy into the world. Joy, what a strange feeling. I felt at times like there would never be any joy anywhere again, but it has come to greet me. I am smiling when I get back to the market.

Liam is outside looking for me. "She is here, inside."

I quit skipping and run the last few steps to the door. Then I remember, Mama said, "Grandmother is a formal person who did not allow us to run or yell even outside." I slow down and try to look what I hope is formal—head erect, shoulders back, breath calm.

Liam bursts into the market shouting, "Here is your surprise! Here she is."

The woman whirls around and looks at me. I see a glimpse of what looks like confusion.

Liam can hardly contain himself. "Mrs. McBride" he says almost properly, except for bouncing, "this is your granddaughter, Mary McCarthy. Mary McCarthy, this is your grandmother, Mrs. McBride."

At first, she just stares into my eyes, head tilted, like she wants to figure something out. Then, straightening, she holds out her hands, "Come here girl."

She holds my hands in hers for a long time, not saying anything at all. This is not how I had imagined it would be. I thought she might swoop me up in her arms like Mama or Da would have. She has never seen me before. Calm. I don't even know if she knew I existed before this very moment. I have been dreaming of her for months, but she left home this morning without the slightest hint anything would be different.

She seems at a loss for words, so I whisper, "Grandmother."

As she continues to stare at me, I have the chance to look at her. She is more hunched than I imagined. Yet, her face looks younger. She has wispy brown hair that escapes from her black hat. Mama never wore a hat, though it's the fashion at home, too. Her eyes, watery and blue like new snow, scare me. Neither her eyes nor her hair remind me of anything like Mama's, still the mouth shaped like a bow and the set of her jaw are identical. She wears some scent mixed with lavender, which makes me queasy.

Dropping my hands, she wraps her black knit shawl tighter around her shoulders even though I do not think it cold today. She takes her wrapped package in one hand and my hand with the other. Without a word, we leave the market.

This is a fine road and the mist has lifted, the seas to the right and mountains on the left. At first Grandmother stays silent. Does she want me here? I can't read her face.

Finally, she stops to look at me, again. "So Mary, what has happened? You did not come here alone because all is well with your mother and father."

I match her cool tone. It will be easier to tell my story if I do not get caught up in the horror of it.

As I tell her the story I get to the part where Da went crazy.

Grandmother hisses under her breath. "I told that girl no good would come if she married a fiddler, but she would not listen. Really though, too old to get a good husband, almost twenty. She was so bullheaded. No one was going to change her mind."

It hurts me that she says that about Da. He was, no is, a wonderful person and a great fiddler. I want to say, we were doing well before he had the accident. I decide against it. There is a chance it would only make her angrier. I just met her. There will be time enough to tell her all my good stories about him.

"One of the constables lifted his rifle and just swung it around so the butt hit Da in the head. Da dropped like a stone. After they threw him in the cart, we never saw him again or heard anything of him."

Mama's good friend wouldn't even open the door all the way. 'They warned us. I can't take you in. They'll destroy our house.' she said" My baby sister, died of cold that night."

I want to shake Grandmother. She does not even appear to care that her own grandbaby died. Is this really my grandmother? I start walking again. Her silence fills me with ice, but I continue.

"We took her to the church. When the Father got there, he said he could help us find a coffin for baby Bridie, then help us with a place we could stay for a little while. He had always thought Mama was special."

Grandmother shakes her head but stays quiet.

"He got his younger sister, a nun of the Poor Clares, to take us in to their convent in Nun's Island. It was in Galway, not a real island. We couldn't stay. Afterwards, Mama said we should come to see you."

I keep rattling on, partly because I am scared. Is Grandmother listening? "Mama and the boys died while Padraig and I were trying to get food."

I sob and hold onto her arm for a minute like a little girl. She pats my back a bit then starts walking again. I wipe my eyes on my sleeve and walk beside her.

"We had to leave them there in a ditch."

119

I hear her take a deep sob, too, but she stops quickly.

"We took a wrong turn. Padraig and I fell into a bog when the road we were on stopped suddenly. That's where Padraig died. I almost did, but I heard a voice. It said I could get up and walk. I think it was God."

She nods so I go on about Mathair and the fairies and my friend. All of it. She just lets me talk and talk. This is the first time I can tell the whole story to anyone. I just want to have someone to listen to me. I am not sure she wants to hear it.

The paved road we are on becomes a dirt trail just past the manor house. She says, "The house belongs to an Englishman who only visits it a month at a time and not every year. He stays most of the time in London and only comes to hunt and have parties. He hires someone who runs the place.

"Our cottage is on his land and there is an overseer who comes and tells us what to plant and what our share will be. All but one of your uncles have gone to work at the shipyards in Liverpool. Thank God for them. We would have not had enough to eat if they hadn't. The lads keep us out of the workhouse."

"Did you know that Liam is from the workhouse?" I ask.

"I am the one who suggested they find a child there, an orphan.

We walk on in silence for a while. Each of us in her own thoughts. We finally get to the gate to her yard. It is lovely, so clean and orderly. Our house never looked this nice. We go inside.

There is an old man in the chair. I think he must be my grandda or maybe my great grandda. My grandmother says softly, "This is her daughter."

I almost say hello to him when he looks me in the eye, spits into the fire and leaves the room. Oh, dear.

He storms back through the room with his coat and hat and roars "What is all this and what are you going to do about it?" That is all. He slams the door and is gone.

Grandmother says "He went out for some air. He will not be back tonight."

I am bewildered. What have I done that he would be so angry the first time he met me? I never even told him my name!

"Would you like a glass of water?"

I nod and she leaves. Sleep has been rare. Even though last night helped, I am more tired than ever. My head jerks up when she sets the water on the table. I realize I was asleep standing. "Grandmother, do you have a place I can sleep for a while."

Grandmother makes a pallet on the floor behind the table and says, "That is an excellent idea. I will wake you when it is time to eat."

I am not quite awake when some women come into the room. Are they my aunts? I have four aunts, my mother's sisters, there are four here. One is with the fairies so there is at least one who isn't a sister. Maybe she is my uncle's wife. I close my eyes quickly when they look my way so that they will think I am still asleep. I am not awake enough to face so many people.

One of them says "I saw a girl in town. I think she is our niece, Katie's daughter." It seems strange she did not come up to me then and introduce herself. She almost whispers to the others, "She has his eyes."

"Oh no." says one with a hoarse voice. "It is no wonder then that I saw our Da storming towards town when I was on my way home."

The one with the nice voice asked, "Whose eyes and why would that matter."

"Sit down and we will tell you about it." Says the first.

"When the overseer was first here, he had his way with a number of the girls and went on to some of the wives. Our mother was one of those unfortunates.

"Some even said that she had encouraged him. Our dear brother, your husband, was one of the worst. He would not talk to Katie ever, and wanted both Mama and Katie put out of the house. He's never softened."

"Did she encourage the overseer?

"No. She most certainly did not. She went out of her way to avoid him. If Da had thought she had, neither mother nor Katie would have ever been allowed under the roof. It almost killed Da just to see those violet eyes and the hair. Every time he saw her, he turned away so he would not lose his temper. That is why he forced her into service so early. She went away and he was almost civil afterwards. I am not sure anyone ever told Katie, but she had to know that he did not want her around. Unfortunately, she lost her position when the family moved, and she was back home."

Another of the aunties pitched in, "I think it is part of why Katie started dancing. When she had a caili to go to she could get away from his angry glances. You know it is how she met her fiddler. It was actually a county fair, not here in County Antrim but south in County Down. She came home with stars in her eyes and told me she had met HIM. When I asked her who and what this 'him' was, she told me about this fiddler. I laughed and said that she should know better than to even think of a fiddler. I said, 'your life will be one misery after the next if you go with him.' Of course, she would not listen to a word of it. Well, you know she was already old by that time. Her prospects were not bright."

"Why?" asked the sister-in-law.

"Why, indeed? Everyone in the area could see her eyes and hair as well as Da could. The boys all wanted her, but their parents would say she would be trouble. Some made even further threats. So, they would marry someone who was not so tainted, and Katie would be left once again. I think it really hurt her to be so rejected. So, when she finally found Michael and he was not about asking permission of his father, she was head over heels."

"Mama begged her not to go with him." said one of the sisters. "Mama even quit talking to Katie when she told her that she was going to marry him with or without their blessing. There were a lot of hard feelings when she left. Katie did have some money and I heard that was what they used to get a start in County Clare. He was actually from County Galway, but I guess there were some hard feelings there too. I am sure it was because he had not asked permission. I heard he did not even tell his family before he brought home an outsider."

"Where did you find out all that?" asked the hoarse one.

"I'm not saying."

"So, Katie got down there and really had no family on his side either. Poor girl. She did nothing to deserve being treated so harshly. I feel sorry for her."

"You haven't heard? Katie is dead. So are four of her five children. The girl is as good as an orphan because to the best of anyone's knowledge her Da was transported for attacking the men who came to evict him. I guess one of them smashed his fiddle and he just went berserk."

"No, I hadn't heard that. So, this girl is here not as a visitor but needs a home?"

"Yes."

"Oh."

Chapter 16:
The Brooch

The brooch is lying on a green wool backdrop. The gold looks old, as if it has been wrapped and unwrapped until it looks almost soft, no longer shiny. It is a gold circle with a long pin.

"What is it, Grandmother?"

"It is a brooch, meant to hold a king's cape. It has come to me from my side of the family. It is ancient. I have kept it hidden since it was given to me by my grandmother."

It is so out of place in this small cottage with its thatched roof and dirt floors. It should be in some castle. Instead it is in Grandmother's worn hand. She holds it as an offering to me.

"Take it. It is all I can give you. Take it and leave."

I am shocked! I can hardly breathe. I cannot speak. Leave? She wants me to go? This is my new home where I am going to be loved and taken care of. Leave?

What is this gold to me? Yet, it has to be the proof Mama told me about. The proof that we were truly of the House of Ulster. Kept out of sight for so long. Passed from grandmother to grandchild. She could have given it to any one of her line. She is offering it to me, a girl, she does not know.

I do not want gold! The roof is what I need, the home. My north star since Mama first told us we would come here. It cannot simply vanish.

She pushes it, the most precious thing she owns, towards me

like there is an urgency about it.

Certainty slaps my heart. Not only must it be accepted, but once I do, it will be the last act of welcome here. To take this will shut the door on this place. The one that should be my new home.

I want to look away. I want to take the brooch and throw it as far as possible. I can do neither. I open my hand, she carefully places it in my palm and closes my thumb over it. More of a ritual than gift. We stand together in silence for a very long time.

Finally, she speaks. "This is the last link that I have to the nobility our family once had. I hope you can keep it always as a reminder of who you are through me and through your mother. I know times are hard. You could possibly get a fair amount of money for this. If that is what must be done, I would not begrudge you. I would have had you stay here. Grow up as my own, but that cannot happen. I have to send you back out into the world even though it breaks my heart."

Her hand drops mine. Her single tear, the only sign of regret.

"You are a beautiful, strong girl. You have nobility in your blood. You will find a way to persevere. I can see it in your eyes. This is the only possession which is mine and mine alone.

"I kept it hidden from those who would have stolen it—my husband, common thieves, and false rulers. I know it will be difficult for you to keep it. If you find that a workhouse is the best solution, and I do know that it is awful to even think about, you should bury it. If you decide that to sell it would keep you out of the workhouse be careful in how you do so. There are those who would accuse you of having stolen it, and then steal it from you. Items of this much value are much harder than those of lesser value to trade."

She stirs the oatmeal in the pot then tells me to sit. The bowl sits untouched. "Eat now. You will regret it later if you miss this food."

I put the spoonful in my mouth, but it has no taste. I swallow, choke it down, then take another bite until the bowl is empty. I feel hollow.

She wraps some oat cakes for the road in a clean cloth. I put them in my apron pocket. Then she opens the door and I step out of the cottage. The dew is still on the grass and chill in the air. She, once again is stern and distant like on the road, says "God be with you."

This all would have been totally unthinkable had I not seen the overseer, had I not heard my aunts talking among themselves. I understand one thing. I am not welcome here.

The gate pushes out easily to let me pass. After one night, I am on the same road but going back the way I came. I have lost my way. Where do I go next?

I speak to the Lord or is it just the air. "Oh God. I am so lost. I do not hear your voice. I do not know which way I am supposed to travel. Please help me, now."

Chapter 17:
Where Next?

I walk until when I look back, I cannot see even the chimney, then sit down in the middle of the path. I take out the pebbles I use as a rosary. No one is here to watch me. I know it is God who told me that I could walk when I was at the end of the road, but right now there are only the sounds of the birds and insects. No answers. The repetition of the prayers comforts me, and I have no other comforts in the world. I start crying. I am overwhelmed. "Hail Mary full of grace…"

I cry until my face feels swollen and my eyes sting. My heart has turned into a stone that drags me to the depths. Once again there is an end to the road, and I have fallen off. This time there is no steady voice to tell me I can walk.

An old woman wrapped in a tattered grey shawl walks towards me. She seems bent by the weight of her basket. As she gets closer, I realize she is the one who told me to stay away from that man, the overseer, my true grandfather. When she reaches me, I nod. I would rather hide. On this windswept hillside there is no other option. I sit, stones in my hands. Maybe she will silently pass me.

"I see things have not turned out as you had hoped."

I do not know if she has known my business here or if it is my sore eyes and face. How my brothers used to tease me and showed no mercy when they knew I had been crying. My breath catches, and I crave to hear a single small voice teasing me now. This woman does not tease.

"No," I say with a bark that sounds like the seals.

She does not push me to say more but waits for me to put away my stones. She motions me with a slight flick of her head.

We walk down the path in silence. I should be thinking about where I will go next but sorrow swallows everything but the grey of her shawl in front of me.

At last my mood lifts a little. The day is cloudy, but it is not raining, just a fine mist. I can sleep outside. There are few travelers in this part of the country. The mountains come up from the sea and if I go high enough there might be a cave or someplace that is a little sheltered. It will be raining before the day is over and the night will wrap me in cold and wet if there is nothing.

I am startled when the woman, still beside me, speaks. "My son, James, is due back tomorrow so you can only stay until then, but you may sleep in my home tonight if you would like to."

I have never heard anything so wonderful in my life, no need to find someplace. Of all the nights ever, to have a roof over my head is an answer to an unspoken prayer.

"Thank you so much." I whisper. "I have some food that I will share with you for supper." After this is gone, I will have trouble getting more, but that is tomorrow's problem.

Her cottage, off of the main road, is almost all the way to town. I understand why when her son gets back, I will need to leave. The shed by the market where I stayed when I first got here was larger and it had no furniture. There are two pallets on the floor made of rags, a box with a bowl on it, and another with clothes in it. There are no windows, only a door.

The thatch on the roof has a patch missing. As it clears and the sun sets, I see two stars through the hole.

I bring out the food and we each eat half of one of the oat cakes. When I suggest that she take more, she shakes her head. "No, I don't need as much as I once did. That was more than enough. Thank you for sharing."

I'm sure she is lying, there was so little. I am glad there is some left, but she could eat every bite. I would not stop her.

After supper, she gets out a small clay pipe. She puts some herbs in it and then lights it by sparking stones. It surprises me to see her puff on it like a man, but it is not my place to say anything. The day is ending, and I realize that she does not have a fireplace nor even a lamp or candle. She bars the door and I hear her make her way back to her bedding. She lets out her breath as she sits. The glow from her pipe is the only light in the room but that is enough when my eyes get used to it. The herbs smell sweet. I recognize them as some to comfort achy joints. The smell reminds me of Mathair and O'Brian, so bittersweet.

She starts her story. "I was just a girl when John Dun, the overseer, first came to the estate. Before him we had a kind old man as overseer. He watched to see that everyone stayed in good health and had enough. When the previous Lord of the estate died, his cousin inherited it. At first, we thought nothing would change, everyone would just go on as they always had since the first.

I was not the prettiest girl in the village, for sure. No one ever bothered me when I did the family's marketing every week. My mother was sick and Da was on his deathbed. We lived out near where your grandmother lives now."

So, she knows who I am.

"I was one of the first to see him. He rode into town on the finest horse I ever saw. Thought it was his, but later found the Lord owned it. His hair was the color of your mother's. Fine gold with just the right amount of red so at the end of sunny days, it was a crown of fire. His strange violet eyes were what took my breath though. I thought, I have never seen a god before, but this must be one.

He called me over to demand to know where the manor was. I was on my way home so I said I could lead him there. I should have just pointed the way.

"You saw it beside the road on the way to your grandmother's. He could hardly get lost. Still, he was so handsome, and he was the new overlord so I thought that I should show him rather than just tell him.

"My life changed from that day. I walked him to the stables as I could take a short cut from there to my house. He did not let me go home. He grabbed me and threw me on the hay and had his way with me. I was not much older than you are. It only happened that once, but it happened. That was how I ended up with my boy, James.

No one would believe me that I did not have a choice. Not until he had done the same to more girls and women around here. Your mother was lucky. She was allowed to grow up in your grandmother's house. There were other women who were like your grandmother who were taken to live in one of the Magdalene asylums and never heard from again. I was more fortunate than them. My brother came and got me and my baby even though he could not convince Da to take me in."

I shudder. I know how it feels to suddenly have no home.

She doesn't notice in the dark. "He helped me get this little cottage. I have made my way by doing sewing and making lace. The others may be still in the laundry of the Magdalenes. They take the babies away, you know. I feel blessed to have James with me." She takes a long draw on her pipe.

I am curious, now. "Did you ever tell the Lord of the manor or anyone who might have had the ability to stop him or at least help support you?"

The old woman laughs. "Oh, you are young," she said. "How could I have reached him? He seldom came to Ireland and would have laughed me out of the county had I been so bold. One girl's father did try to talk with him on one of his rare visits. He was told to pack up, and leave the area, because his daughter had brought shame to the estate. There was never going to be any relief from that man." She stopped to tap the ashes out of her pipe and refill and light it. The only light was a pale sliver of moon.

It took her a long time. I thought maybe she was tired, but she started again when the glow from her pipe was steady. "My son never did find a girl who would marry him, so he lives here with me. He is older than your mother. I was so happy when she found your father and left this place. I knew how bad it would be for her here. I guess it did not turn out as well as I had hoped when she left, but who could have known the whole country would be in ruins like it is now. It should have been a great place for her. She loved your father so much."

I feel so comfortable with her. I want to know more about my real grandfather. "My mama got so she could not hold her drink. She would go crazy if she did not have some. When she got more, she would become mean. Was John Dun like that?"

"Yes, he was, still is. It got worse and worse over the years. He was not bad the day you arrived, but some days he is in a rage and hurts people when they have done nothing. Around here the girls and women go out only in groups or with their grown sons or husbands. Everyone except your grandmother that is. I don't know why she is so bold. However, she does use a shillelagh for a walking stick. I think it is against the law, but no one has questioned her yet. If she killed him, they would all be sure she was to blame."

Maybe he should be killed. It might not be so easy to tell who did it. I could. No, remember how it was when Da went crazy. I just cannot think about this now. I bring myself back to the old woman who is talking on about her son now. I am sorry he has had such a hard life.

"It is time now that we need to be getting some rest. I will keep my pipe going while you make yourself cozy there."

Now, I am almost too excited to sleep. My head is spinning with all the things that have happened. I never expected to be here in this hovel with a strange woman who tells me more about who I am than I got from my own mother or grandmother. I don't even know her name and she can tell me my grandmother's whole history and my mother's too.

At least I now know a lot of why my mother had never thought we should travel to see her family. Not that the roads were so easy even when everything was better. I always thought she would have mentioned about going to see her family. With a start, I realize she did not know if we would be welcomed when we set out. She was more desperate than I knew.

When Mama said we would go to Grandmother's house, she gave us no hint there might be a problem. I thought when we got here, we would find a happy homecoming, to a family who would welcome us into their house and hearts.

I wonder what she thought she would do when she got here. Did she have some kind of plan or was she past caring? I cannot even imagine showing up here with the whole family. I doubt we would have been allowed in the door.

Why am I trying to keep my eyes open? It is totally dark in here. I close my eyes and Bridie, my baby sister is in front of me. Oh God. Please take her into your arms and make her safe and warm. I am given a sense of peace. Bridie disappears.

Chapter 18:
Not Here!

I must be in a hand cart. Every small bump on the road jolts my back, while my feet dangle before me over the front of the cart. Desperate, I pull myself out of horrible dreams of being on a ship tossed by waves. My stomach rolls with each step. The urge to vomit is how I know I'm not dead. Does the person pushing me think I am? I need to talk before he throws me into a pit. I attempt to say, hello. It comes out as "huh."

"Oh, good afternoon. A man said you were as good as dead, and I shouldn't waste my time with you. I didn't believe him. You were delirious for a long time and hot as a fire when I touched you. I did wonder if you would make it."

He stops pushing the cart. A face peers down at me. He looks like a younger version of the old woman, except the violet color of his eyes. James, maybe? Good, no certainty I won't end up in a pit, but with him I have a chance. How long has it been? It seems like we have been on the road forever. Most pits are nearby.

After I clear my throat, I find I can speak. "I had strange dreams. My dead brothers all had pointed teeth. They chased me around a ship so they could bite me. I knew I had to get away from them or I would die. I ran and ran. Did I scream out loud? My throat hurts.

"At last, Mama came. She did bite me. Strange new creatures covered in hair and smelling like smoke grabbed me with long claws. Was it you? Who are you? Where are we? Where are you taking me?"

"I am James. I guess I am an uncle on our father's side. Mum and I put you in the cart together. We are on the road to the workhouse in Belfast. "

"No. Please no. I don't want to die."

"I am not taking you there to die," he laughs. "They have a sanatorium, a place for the sick, where you can rest and get something to eat. My mum and I have no way of taking care of you. We have no food, and not even space for you on the floor. If we had either, but no, you need help and we can't give it to you."

"They are awful places. Everyone told me horrible stories. Bad food, sometimes no food, beatings, many dying."

"I can let you out of the cart right here if you want."

"Yes."

I try to stand as he helps me out of it, but I am weaker than I thought. If he leaves me here, I will just fall down and die. Fear shoots through me.

"You're right. Put me into the cart." It is very bumpy, but exhausted, I drift in and out of sleep.

The next time I wake, I am in the line to the workhouse. I keep my eyes closed. It smells salty here like maybe we are near the coast. Over everything is the reek of the dying, which terrifies me.

James explains to a worker. "I am not her father. My mother says she is kin, but I am not sure how."

He knows he is my uncle, but I stay quiet for once. I want to have James get me past this person before I open my eyes.

With a sneering voice she says, "I will have to look on the local records to see if she is qualified to be here. What's her name?"

"Mary O'Neill"

I don't know why he has lied, my name is not O'Neill. Maybe it is because it is common here, and I would not be on the parish rolls in this county.

She must be satisfied because the cart starts rolling.

"Thank you, James." I whisper. I don't know if he hears me.

They take me into the sanatorium, undress me, and start to put me into a shift. I suddenly remember the brooch. I had put it into the hem of my dress.

I slip my hand through my clothes, but it is not there. Where is it? I panic but try not to show it.

They will take it away and accuse me of stealing if they find it before I do. Where is it? Did I drop it on the road or in the cart? Worse yet, did James take it from me? It is not here.

I lay my head back. Heat consumes me. My mouth is parched. If I could cry right now, I would. My heart breaks. I thought I did not want it, but it is my only tie to my family.

It is much worse inside the main room. It turns my stomach, so many people dying of diseases, injuries, as well as starvation. I have found hell.

A young lady with a bucket of water brushes by me.

"Water, please." My voice comes out as a croak.

She only has a common cup. The water she drips into my mouth tastes like the nasty bucket they keep it in. She pours the water into my mouth. To swallow is my only option. She takes the sheets from a dead person to put on me. I could have died on the road in the clean mist. Why did I come here? She moves on.

An old woman lifts my head and spoons a liquid into my mouth. It takes me a bit to recognize it is a thin gruel of oatmeal and something else. She also gives me some buttermilk a drop at a time. It is good. Helps with the fire in my body.

If I were not this sick and hungry, the strange taste in the oatmeal would make my stomach heave. Right now, it is the best food I have ever eaten.

I start shivering but I do not know if it is the room or the fever.

135

There are no blankets. The rain outside makes a soft music which seems out of place here. I wish for Mama.

I am not sure I can make it. "God, I commend my life into your hands." I cannot hear my own voice.

****

I bathe in sweat but feel like I may live. A man prepares to bleed me. Just then, a woman across the room goes into fits. He doesn't get back to me. I am grateful.

I can now sit on my pallet and eat on my own. I have listened for several days. I think Miss O'Brian was right. The bleeding hurts rather than helps. The worst was a young mother. I thought she would be fine. She was starting to talk to her baby, but after being bled she drifted away. They took her body out this morning. I pray for her soul and her poor baby. Thank You, God, for sparing me from bleeding.

****

Better now, I am moved into new quarters. The matron grabs me by an ear. "You worthless, little street urchin. You are lucky we took you in, should have died out on the street."

My prayers are my only comfort. I lost the pebbles I used to use to say the rosary. I have to pay attention, but I can say the right number of prayers if I use my fingers. Even then I lose my place sometimes. James was right, this was the only place I would be fed and housed but oh, I wish for a better place.

I start singing the lament I heard from Mathair. Here, with all of these people, I feel more alone than ever before. "I'm so alone, I'm so alone…."

A girl shouts, "Hush up there."

I hum under my breath so quietly no one but God can hear.

I had a better bed on the grass out under the stars. The wooden pallets with a little scratchy straw are overcrowded. Every day there are more bug bites. For sure, we had a few in our little thatched house and in the stable. These make me itch from head to toes. It is maddening. I miss home.

I miss O'Brian, too. I thought of a problem with our experiment and I would like just one more chance to read his books, especially Mary Somerville's. What does it matter now? The experiment is over.

The walls are cold grey stone in our dormitory. I smell the sour sickness and the sweet-horrible odor of the dead from the sanatorium. Mama would have had a fit if she were here. I smile. At least she is not here telling me how miserable she is, as if I could fix it. Tears sneak out the corners of my eyes.

I find out tomorrow what my work will be. Only the desperately sick are allowed to go without a job. I can do some basic stitches, hopefully there is sewing work they need done. It is mostly that or work in the kitchen for the girls who stay here.

The kitchen girls return to our rooms exhausted, burned, and covered in grime. Maybe, I'll be sent outside to a factory or a manor. There were several girls who were mangled or lost fingers who came into the sanatorium from the weaving factory. A tiny girl had hair and part of her head caught in a machine. Oh God, please do not let me be sent there.

Exhaustion almost catches up with me when a girl plops down on the pallet beside me. Her red curly hair escapes her headscarf.

I'm tired and weak. Talking seems like a lot of work, so I don't. Unfortunately, she has already seen my eyes open.

"Hello, I'm Ginny. You're new here. They told me your name is Mary. I suppose this is the first time you've been in the dormitory. I know we are crowded with six of us on the pallet, but you'll get used to it. One time there were eight of us here.

"I was scared when I got here, they would make me into a scullery maid or something else even harder. The matron put me to sewing, all mending and such. The women work on clothes from here and do work brought in from the outside. She says I am not ready for those, but I don't care.

"I would be fine if they let me see Mama more than once a week. She is a cook's helper. I just see her on Sundays for a little while. She complains the whole time. 'The work is terrible. Look at all the burns on my arms. Remember how beautiful my hands were. They'll never be the same.' She goes on and on."

I think like mother like daughter.

"She blames Da for our low state. Da sometimes does not come to see us when he could. I think he is ashamed. They beat him, tell him he's worthless. At first, he came to see us, but Mama cried the whole time. Now he just stays in his quarters."

Will this girl ever quit? To stop her, I ask, "Do you have the Gaelic."

She says "No, but if you do, I would not use it. They think we are plotting something if they hear it. It is no longer illegal in this country but do not speak it here. They do not whip us, well, the men get it, but you might go without food.

"They slap us for sport of course, but it is worse if they have what they call "cause". I have been in solitary twice, once just for talking. It is bad. They put me in a dark room which was bad enough but when a rat ran across my foot the first time, I screamed and screamed. No one came to check me. I promised myself I would never go back after the first time. The second was when I sewed the front into the back of the skirt by accident while reattaching the waistband. It wouldn't have taken any time to fix it. You should have heard the words she used."

I wish I had let James leave me to die by the road, still here I am. I will have to watch for my chance to get out of this place. I hate rats.

I close my eyes and hope she will stop. She continues. "Sometimes when someone breaks a big rule, they take away supper for everyone for a week. They look for any excuse to punish us when the food is short. Mama has told me sometimes they come back from trying to get food with barely anything. It is mean, but they pick one of us and say they are the reason for short rations.

"Some of the people here do not get it. They think they are being punished for what someone did instead of it just being no food. "They found one man dead after he was made the scapegoat."

Finally, I say, "I need to get some sleep now if I can. I still feel very weak."

She turns to the girl on the other side of her and starts whispering until the matron opens the door. I have never been more glad in my life to see someone in authority. I think once she quits talking, it will be quiet, but it is not.

There are two little girls not much older than my littlest brothers who came into the workhouse today with their family. No one told them the family would be split apart into the men's, women's, boys', and girls' sections. They had always been with their mama. At first, they think their mama will come soon and cry for her. When they realize she isn't going to come, they sob even louder. I hurt to hear them.

I fear the matron will come back into the room and punish all of us. Relief. An older girl lies down with them and starts singing a soft lullaby. At first, they ignore her, but eventually let themselves be calmed.

How will I ever get away?

Chapter 19:
Is This the End?

5:00 AM. Still dark outside, the time we wake up each morning. The matron comes in and calls out the time at the top of her lungs. She seems like she is miserable and bent on making us the same.

The new little girls get startled every day and start crying. At first my heart went out to them, but I am beginning to harden to their wails and only find it annoying. Am I becoming a heartless person like the matron?

I got the job my friend most feared, scullery maid, which means to wash out the giant pots, where the porridge is cooked on like glue. All I'm given is a soapy cloth and sand.

The cook yells at least every other day, "You lazy, good for nothing girl. This pot is filthy. No supper for you. Now, polish it until it shines. If I have to say it again, you'll get a beating."

Sometimes there is a little food to scrape off with my fingernails and eat. I go without food often enough, but she has yet to hit me.

I also scrub floors on my knees and clean until everything in the kitchen is spotless. When I am fed, it is only a watery gruel of whatever they could get. The work starts early and ends late at night with never enough sleep. Some of the other women kick me and one dumps my soapy water everywhere if I am not quick enough to get it out of her way. I have never done anything to her.

My friend says some of the people here are mean for sport. I think back to the man who shattered Da's fiddle, I guess that kind of person may be all too common. I hope I am not beaten down until I turn into one of them. I fear I might be.

The days are running into one another now, each one the same. I look forward to the start of school. When Da or Mama used to teach me, I thought learning was the best thing ever. I spent hours trying to learn to write the Gaelic with the flowing letters Da used. We did not have paper and pens, so I would scratch it onto a rock with a stick and wash it with water and start over again.

It is my first day in class, finally. I pick up my chalk with my left hand, pain—quick and sharp causes me to drop it.

The schoolmaster hits me with a stick again and yells, "You devil's spawn. You will not be using that evil hand here. I will break you of your papist ways, by God."

I will never be able to write the beautiful way I once did if forced to use my right hand. It is a terrible problem. He does not let me use my left hand for anything. I am like a baby, trying to relearn everything with my right hand.

The matron comes by my pallet each night. I want to ask her if I can sew with Ginny, but I have been too afraid. I used to help Mama with the mending and was learning to make the tiny stitches which did not show.

Tonight, with all my courage, I blurt out, "Can I help sew? I learned how from my mother and I can do it well."

To my surprise, the matron says, "You can show me tonight if you think you are good."

Without a thought, the wrong hand lifts the needle. She grabs the cloth away from me before I take my first stitch, then cuffs my ear hard enough to make it ring. Even sleep escapes me, as the pain and noise combine.

The scullery was extra hard today. As I cry myself to sleep, a friend reaches over and pats my back. I know some people have found ways, other than dying, to leave. Something has to work for me.

In the yard after chapel, I look around. It is a beautiful day, but it does not brighten my spirit. Those of us who do not have their mamas here, stay together in one part of the yard while more fortunate, leave to visit. This is always the low point of my week. Mama could yell and be crazy all she wanted to if I could just be with her and touch her hands once a week. She would be crazy here, since there is no drink, and they have so many rules. Still, right now, I would give anything to spend just a few minutes with her.

My friend rushes to me across the yard. She is all smiles. "We are going to America." She shouts before she even is near. "My da got put on an outside roads project." She bounces like she would start to dance if it were permitted. "We are going to America!" She repeats.

I heard her the first time. I thought it could not get worse, but here it is. She is going to America, and I will stay here. One tear escapes my eye before I can stop it.

"Oh, sorry. I did not think. You are not coming to America with me. I am sorry, it is just Mama was thrilled when she was telling me, and I got so excited. I just wanted to tell you, as my best friend. Now you look so sad and I cannot make it better."

I wipe my eyes and imitate a smile. "This is wonderful. I am so glad for you. I will be fine here. I will find my own way to America someday. Then we can meet, and we will be fine ladies and have tea and crumpets and you will tell me all of what has happened to you and I will tell you the whole story of how I made it out of here. We will tell our children about how we met and laugh about how hard it was."

Part of me feels like this is the most embroidered tale I have ever told her, but a tiny part of my heart thinks it could be the truth. Well, maybe not the part about meeting again, I know it would be hard to find each other.

"Wait, I have an idea. When Mama and my family were first evicted, we stayed with the Sisters in the Poor Clare convent on Nuns Island in Galway. We could also try writing to the workhouse, here. I will write both places when I arrive. You do the same when you get to a place you can write and wait for an answer. One of them might do it. It possibly would help if we each sent some money to help the Poor Clares. I would not send a penny to the workhouse, but they might help, anyway. Those two are our only hope. Please remember."

"I promise I will. You just have to find a way to get there, too, and someday we will get together and laugh."

"Don't forget, if you can, send them a donation. They saved us then and they have little themselves. They were lovely and so generous."

****

The dream of America keeps me alive now. If I did not have any hope, I would have lost everything. No, I have to be honest with myself. I have three things that help me survive and the dream is for sure one of them. The next is the voice who I believe is God. Finally, it is the knowledge that I have the blood of kings. I would rub the brooch if I could; to remind myself. Since I no longer have it, I will rub the memory of it in my mind.

Some days even with those, it is all I can do to get out of bed when the matron yells, "Five o'clock, everyone up! Five o'clock!" It used to scare me so much I would leap up. I wish it scared me today. I would like to feel the surge of energy. Now I feel like I am at least a hundred years old and my bones, a thousand. My hands once pretty, hurt and are rough because of this work.

I excel at school when it does not include writing, but I was so tired the other day, I picked up my chalk with the wrong hand. My chance at supper disappeared because of one small motion. I find the one thing I was most proud of has become my ruination.

Chapter 20:
Escape?

Another day, like most of the previous ones is interrupted by an order to come into the matron's office. I must have done something wrong, but right now I have no idea what. This is not the first time I have not known what was wrong. I harden myself for some hungry days at best and the rat cave at the worst.

No one else calls it the cave but being there reminds me of the time I spent in the cave where I got the salts with Kalen. I was so terrified then. Now, I have some of the same sorts of visions. Never the ones I had the first time. New ones. The thought of Kalen brings a smile to my heart. How is he fairing now?

I open the door with dread. There is a line of children in the office. Several more girls enter after me. I am surprised to see a very elegant lady who I think might be English. She watches each girl as she enters.

The matron starts going down the line explaining what each of us has been doing and our overall attitude. Some of the girls are dismissed immediately for having been uncooperative, some only for looking too downcast. I don't know what the matron will say about me. I also don't know if I want to be picked or dismissed. It doesn't matter, we are supposed to stand straight and not say anything. Whatever I have done, good or bad, is already done. I can only stand here.

The second time down the row the lady asks questions about

each of us. "Has she ever been in service before? What does she know about household matters? What is her work here? Is she neat, can she read and write? How quickly had she adapted to the routines of the workhouse? Is she always on time?" The matron answers, politely to her repeated questions.

She is not English but perhaps Italian. She makes comments to herself in some foreign language. Turning to the matron she says, "I have decided to staff the manor with people from the workhouse. I want discretion above all. I appreciate your choice of the housekeeper. I assume the rest will be of her caliber."

The matron nods then holds a chair for her, and motions for her to sit.

The lady is relentless. "I want the Irish. Of course, servants in Italy are naturally much better at everything. Be sure they have no English connections!"

My guess about her language is correct. Inwardly, I smile while I keep my dull outward appearance.

"I did not know when I married my husband how backwards his England is. And Ireland! I am furious he would make me come to a total backwater like this."

One girl rolls her eyes at the wrong moment.

Matron growls at her. "You are dismissed. I will deal with you later." As the girl left, the matron turned on us. "Is there anyone else who feels she knows more than her betters?" she asks. None of us says a word.

I look straight ahead, but some of the others look at their shoes. They too are dismissed. The lady starts questioning the matron about us again. She lines us up from tallest to smallest. I am at the end of the line.

Next, she pulls out of line the girls who do not look as neat as possible in the uniforms. I am lucky, my hair is straight and takes little care to keep in order, others with curly hair are dismissed

146

because their hair is unruly.

Finally, the lady stands, and goes down the line stating what position each of us will hold—a lady's maid, three housemaids, two cooks' helpers and last me, the scullery maid.

Scullery maid again! I hide my feelings and stare straight ahead. I try to feel grateful. Here I am finally getting out of this workhouse. It is possibly the first step on the journey I hope to take—to America. I daydream for just a second and only by luck feel the hand of the girl next to me brush mine as she turns to leave. We are dismissed and sent directly to the wagon.

As we leave, the matrons says, "There is no need to tell anyone goodbye or collect anything. You will only be on a two month assignment. Then you will be back here at the workhouse."

They turn, and I hear the lady say, "Now for the men and boys."

My heart drops. I was hoping I could start low and then work my way up to housemaid or nanny like Mama had been. Two months is not nearly enough time to do what I need. It is not even enough time to earn money to go to America. Maybe, it will at least be easier to escape.

We are taken directly to a wagon in front of the workhouse. Several of the other girls complain as we walk because we have not even had time to go to the privy. No one is listening. I reach the door of the workhouse and look towards the wagon. I freeze.

The violet eyes of the man, the man who is my actual grandfather, stare blankly at us. Fortunately, his attitude seems to be more—this is taking entirely too much time out of my day. He keeps looking at the sun and then the road. He does not help us up the ladder to get into the wagon. We will be sitting on some straw on the floor. I find a space in the wagon over the wheels. I do not want to be too far forward nor too far back, just stay invisible in the middle.

I like the smell of the hay and the feel of the warm, light mist. This is the first time I have been away from the workhouse and its horrible stench for months. I have lost track of time. I do not even know how old I am anymore.

The men and boys, who will also be in service, join us. We are off. The lady's coach passes us on the road. We are left to be hauled like farm animals back to the manor. I am happy being one of the animals today. Baa.

The road back to the manor is long. John Dun is what James' mama called him. Dun means dark. His skin is not dark, just his heart. Too bad he is my grandfather. He finally decides he needs to relieve himself and stops the cart. The girls around me almost fight to be the first down the ladder. He finishes his business quickly and then stands watching the bushes like he is imagining each girl.

The day is bright and a warm, but I shiver when I see him look my friends over. A few do not leave as they could not stand the bumping and relieved themselves in the hay on the wagon floor. I feel sorry for them.

I have to go and do my business, or I will join those in puddles. I do not meet his gaze. Shame fills me. My own grandfather has so little heart. He seems like the kind who would eat his own children for the sport of it. I will do my best not to let him know I am related to him in any way. There is no doubt he would and could harm me. At least I know enough to stay away from him as much as possible.

The rain gets very heavy and the sky dark. No wonder he was in a hurry to get back on the road. We are given some oat cakes and water to drink. The oat cakes stick in my throat, so I sip the water. I am careful about how much. This trip could take a long time.

It has gotten very late. We probably will make it all the way to the manor before we stop again. There are few houses and none that look like they would welcome us along this road. Except when I was in the marshes, this is the most isolated part of Ireland I have seen.

The rain finally stops. The cold wind dries my clothes, but my teeth chatter. Most of us stare up at the stars. A few curl their arms around their knees and sleep. The towns we pass are small. The wagon is so crowded. I would love to be on foot where it would be possible to sleep on the side of the road.

The places to sit by the edges of the wagon are filled. My body is sore from sitting. I think I may even be getting some blisters on my backside. Still, the moon is bright, and I hear the waves and smell the ocean like I did at home every night.

When we do stop, I get my first space again. It feels wonderful as I ease my back. Then the woman who will be head housekeeper speaks. "You are in my seat. Move."

Already we are being turned from nearly equals into domestics who know their proper place. Of course, I give in, I do not want to get crosswise with someone who can turn the next two months into a living hell. She has the air of one who has been waiting for the chance to get at someone. I pray there will be a way to get a better position.

Chapter 21:
Once a Scullery Maid...

We stand in a bedraggled line, all of us exhausted. The butler inspects us. By his bearings and his accent, he is from England. Apparently, our new master, Lord Marborough, did not feel the need to use the workhouse to get his staff, like he made his wife do. I should not even think that way. It is above my station.

In front of a manor in a night so black I can see little more than the butler, as fine mist soaks our clothes, I shiver uncontrollably. On our way here, we had no rest and little food. The chill keeps me from falling asleep at least.

We listen to him say in his proper British accent, "You will have to follow a list of rules which will be provided to the housekeeper for the girls. The cook will inform the kitchen help. I will inform the male staff, personally. You will learn these. Ignorance of them will not be an accepted excuse. Each of you will be docked your first week's wages for new clothes, with a few exceptions."

I hear several very small groans. Past caring, I just hope this will end, and we will be allowed to go to our beds soon.

The butler continues, "Your wages will be docked for every infraction. No quarter will be given. I run a tight ship here."

Is this the real reason we are here? Are they planning on getting our labor for nothing?

The cook leads me, alone, to a room up four narrow flights of stairs. Not only is she not out of breath, she talks continuously the entire way.

"You will have a room by yourself. You will rise before dawn. Since there are no windows, I will ring the bell to let you know when. There will be no contact with the Lord, Lady, or any guest. If one of them makes any contact with you, get me immediately. Avoid the male staff except in the common room, then be as discreet as possible. You will..."

As we finally reach my room she is still talking, but it has become like the sound of the ocean at night. Almost asleep, I walk into the tiny room, shake my head enough to hear what I hope is the last of her for tonight.

"You will do what I tell you without argument or question. Ask me, if you want to go to the privy. You do know how to use a privy? I hear tell locals use the roadside to to their business. You have a chamber pot for night which you will empty."

I nod as she speaks, then look where she points at a large brown mug with a broken handle. It is caked with evidence of past use and gives the room an evil odor. Right now, falling asleep is all I care about.

"Don't think these are all the rules. Your clothes will be acceptable for our work. You will not be docked the first week like the rest."

Other than the smell it reminds me of our cottage at home, but it was roofed in thatch. These are shingles nailed to boards, and in a few places, the rain drips through in puddles. It explains the odd placement of the pallet. Thatch is much tighter. At the thought of home and how nice it was, a dull ache spreads through my heart.

There is no one else in my room. I thought I would be with someone, I miss the company. As I take off my dress, Cook, who had gone into the hall, startles me by stomping back towards my room, grumbling. I hold my dress to cover my body. Is she talking to me?

"The lady is not happy at having to have a good English cook. I am well renowned in my town. No. She wants some Italian chef, but the Master put his foot down. He did. He's a good man, he is." Then she rattles the latch but does not open the door, turns, and stomps away.

Maybe, the Lord and Lady Marborough are not as well off as they look from the outside. None of my affair, nor is it any of the cook's.

I stay quiet, hoping she is really gone. She continues to mumble, and I hear her feet stomp down the steep stairs.

Naturally, Cook took the oil lamp. In the blackness, I recite the rosary and say prayers for the souls of my family and a special one for Da's safety. At least since I am alone, there is no one to tell me not to say them out loud. I doubt I would finish if the prayers were silent.

A bell in my dreams is ringing insistently. NO, not my dreams. I jump up and scurry to put my workhouse clothes back on, glad for once to wear my ragged dress. I give a tug on the bell string, so she knows I am coming, run down the stairs, and into the kitchen.

Cook says, "You will have to learn how to get dressed quickly. You must get to the kitchen when I ring the first time. You don't think I put kettles on the fire."

I may have to wear my dress when I sleep. I am used to getting myself to my job early. I hope soon I can wake before the bell. I would rather not sleep in my filthy dress. It was such a short night. I dare not argue my case, and simply say, "Yes, ma'am," as I did at the workhouse.

Cook says, "Don't you be ma'aming me. Cook is good enough. I won't be going above my station and neither should you. You will be called Eliza."

"But my name is Mary."

"Why should I waste my time learning every new name? I never have been in a house where it was different, above or below stairs. It is Eliza now and you will be docked for talking back to me. Never back talk! You hear?"

"Yes, Cook."

I hate the name Eliza but the first day Cook uses it without end. "Eliza, boil some water. Eliza, clean this pot, Eliza! Eliza! Eliza!" Fighting her will not help, I respond to endless calls for Eliza, still, each time I shout in my head—Mary! Mary! Mary!

The work is the same as what I have been doing for months, but there is no schooling here. I miss it, no matter how hard it was writing with my right hand.

Cook yells, "Eliza, where is the pot I asked for? No daydreaming on the job."

I jump. I have to pay attention to this boring work, or she will dock my pay. I am glad I know about being a scullery maid from the workhouse. I can do this and unless I let my mind wander, everything will be fine. It is worse for the girls who go above stairs.

The butler has started instructing them in the hall by the room where I work. I never know what I will need to know in the future, I listen while they are learning. He repeats the rules over many times. I now know the ones for each position.

I don't think the poor lady's maid has made two pence in wages. She is constantly doing something wrong and is being docked. I saw her crying when she thought no one was looking. It is one job I would never want.

On the other hand, the housemaids go without lectures except on the topic of fireplaces, now. The master has brought his own wood for fires instead of using the good peat of Ireland. The housemaids being Irish have no idea how to lay a fire with wood or how to light it.

Every morning, I hear the butler explain it. Every night, he says,

"Are you daft girls? You do not lay nor light the fire correctly. You will have to clean the walls and curtains daily until you can do this without making a mess, and I am docking your wages until you get it right!"

While I am in the pantry putting up the remains from the morning meal, I hear something very large put on our worktable. I peek out and see Cook in full steam descend on the butler. He has on a white apron which is black from whatever it is he put on my clean space. Cook has a butcher knife in her hand and by her looks would like to serve butler for dinner.

"What do you mean by putting that filthy brazier on my clean table?" She snarls.

With a voice like the first gust off the North Atlantic, he replies, "I am your superior here. Remember your place or you will be out the door with no way back to England!"

Cook does not put down the knife but stands back. I no longer think she will use it on him, but she might. Finally, she goes to the pantry, gets the eel she plans to cook for dinner, and chops off the head with such force, the knife sticks in the cutting board.

Not only has he put a brazier on the granite table where we cook, but also has a groom dump an armful of dry wood onto it. From my hiding place I see Cook scowl. I hope the butler or at least his groom cleans the mess. Otherwise, it will be me.

The butler demonstrates how to lay the wood properly then how to light it. I am fascinated. The wood does put out a lovely warm heat and the flames dance, still, I would miss the dark earth smell of a good peat fire.

After he finishes, he smothers it with a tight lid then has each housemaid demonstrate. One has trouble lighting it. He patiently works with her until I want to jump out of the pantry and hold her hands, so she does it right.

The groom does a poor job of cleaning. Does he think I have

extra time to clean after their mess? I fume as he leaves.

Without a word, Cook drags me out of the pantry by an ear, shoves a steamy washcloth in my hand and stomps back to stir the soup. Feeling blessed she did not do worse to me, I scrub the table until it shines.

****

I am in the scullery when I hear the housekeeper's flat voice. "Come here Jane. I saw you looking up as our house guest, Corporal Baker, walked past today."

Jane, who is always respectful, answers, "Yes, Mrs. Brown."

"If I see you do such a thing again, I will dismiss you on the spot. Do you understand?"

I am shocked to hear such a harsh rule.

"Yes, Mrs. Brown." Then silence is restored.

I knew we were not supposed to speak to anyone above stairs, the men in particular. I am horrified. We should not even look a man in the face? It would be hard for me. I was taught as a girl to look my elders in the eye and it would be disrespectful to only look at their shoes.

A few days later she is not at dinner with the rest of the servants. The butler announces, "Jane was dismissed for unbecoming conduct. Let this be a lesson to you all. Inappropriate behavior will not be tolerated. Her replacement is a trained girl, who will be called Jane. Please welcome her when she arrives."

Cook was not lying. It must be policy to have names by position. It makes me feel a little better. Still, who chose Eliza? Such a name!

I am not sure what really happened to the first Jane, but one of the other housemaids calls it fraternizing. It is an unfamiliar word. I only hear it once. I am embarrassed to ask questions, although I do not know why. The ones who know more, say nothing when I am around.

I am glad it is easy for me to stay far from the gentlemen. I thought I had the worst position in the manor, now I think it is the best. It is, except for the heavy, hot work, lack of windows, and paltry pay.

Chapter 22:
Outings

Freedom! My first day since James put me in the workhouse. Not only a day in town, but real coins and the delightful choice to save or spend it. The Lord and Lady have gone on a hunt at another estate. Even Cook will be with us.

Annie, the newest housemaid, is in the corner crying softly. I suppose between demerits and a fancy uniform, she did not get any of her wages. I hope she will at least join us in going to town. It's such a pretty day.

I sit beside her and whisper, "My purse will be as closed as if it had nothing in it. Join us, just for the outing."

Annie smiles, wipes her face.

I tell her, laughing, "Where I am from, we never used money. My first ever was from a woman whose daughter I helped. Bought some Indian corn, made me sick to my stomach. Not too sure if I like this new cash, but it is how things are done here."

She makes a little half smile then says, "So many are going into town to see what they can buy with their coins. I admit, I am jealous, and was ready to stay here and miss everything. Thank you."

In the kitchen, there is no one but Cook and I. She grumbles as she makes breakfast for us, and packs food for a picnic. "Here everyone else is fancy free, and I am still working."

I do not mention the fact I am doing the worst parts. No use in riling her up more. I am glad to have Annie's company today. I will give Cook a wide berth.

At last the dishes are washed and the baskets are packed. I find Annie outside and we walk together.

"Annie, you were not in the workhouse when I got my position. Are you from there or did you get your place from outside?"

"My family just went into the workhouse and I was sent out the next day. I miss my family."

"You would have missed them anyway unless you have a sister. Families are split. There is only one short visit a week, and they delight in taking that away for breaking any rule."

"So how did you end up here, Eliza."

I wince but do not correct her. "I came from the workhouse, too. Before that, I came from a little town near the mouth of the Shannon River. I walked to near here.

"In all of my travels, I never thought how much I would miss being able to walk. To see the green of the countryside and hear the birds is like a miracle. I hope one of these days I can leave the workhouse. When you get some money, what would you like to buy?"

Annie looks off to the clouds rolling through the sky, then speaks in a low voice. "What I really want is a big yellow ribbon to tie my hair. It seems silly, but I saw a girl looking out a carriage window in Belfast with a ribbon like that. She was quickly pulled back into her seat, but I thought she was the most lovely thing I ever saw."

"I used to dream of buying something, too. I have become so practical these days. For a long time, I thought about getting a hat. My skin gets burnt but not as bad as some I've seen. Still, if I have my sights on getting away to America, I have to save every bit of money I get. I don't know what my chance is, but it would be a sad day if I were short only a few pence for my fare. I refuse to spend anything."

She sticks out her lower lip and whines, "At least you got wages. I got demerits and a dress they will not let me keep according to Bonnie, oops, Jane. I can't believe they don't even allow us our names. It costs nothing."

We fall into silence.

At the market, I see Liam. I want to ask him how he has been. I want to tell him everything that has happened to me, but he is with customers. There is also some worry about fraternizing. I don't want to accidentally do what the first Jane did, so they send me away.

The market smells so good I close my eyes and let the odors of cheese, breads, and apple fill my head. I am startled when Liam says, "May I help you." Then he laughs when I jump.

I look around but do not see Cook or the housekeeper. Liam asks, "So, you are at the manor now? The shop is different from the last time you were here."

He sticks his chest out like he has important information. "We always try to have more in stock when Lord Marborough is near." Then in a hushed voice says, "They don't tell us when they're coming. My folks ordered too much one time. The Lord and Lady don't shop here, just servants. The toffs get what they need from London or even Italy."

"I never heard that word. Toffs, was it?"

"Oh, I just learned it the other day. Means the Lord and Lady. I thought it was a grand word."

"It is."

I want to talk with him more, but Liam has to wait on ones who are ready to pay. The footman buys tobacco for his pipe, and several of the girls buy ribbons.

Annie finds me and points at Cook, who must have been outside earlier. She whispers, "She looks like she would like some of the tobacco, too. Did you hear there is a strict rule? None of the female staff may smoke or chew. I'll wager she 'forgets' something and has to come back to get the tobacco."

"They did not tell our group about tobacco." I say. "I would not want it anyway. It stinks."

"They only told me some of the rules, too. Most of my demerits are for the ones they missed."

"Anyway," I tell her, "I would not take that bet. Sometimes Cook smells of smoke when she has been to the privy. I don't think she gets demerits because they had a hard time finding someone who can actually cook at a price they want to pay. Cook regularly tells me how underpaid she is."

"Are any of us paid enough?" Annie snorts. "But she is a decent cook."

"She does deserve more. I used to think about working my way up to being a cook. Not now! The heat is brutal in the kitchen even when it's a cool day. I would rather become something like a housemaid, like you. I am quick and would do a better job than some of the ones in the manor. Besides, you get to see the whole house. I envy you. Just to get the chance to look out the windows! The ones in the kitchen are so high, I see only sky. The scullery and pantry do not have a single window, the scullery only gets light from the kitchen. I even look forward to going to the privy but cook scowls if I go too often. There has to be some better position."

Annie nods her head but says nothing.

On the way back to the manor, I see the new Jane. She seems to know more than the rest of us. I pull Annie's arm to get her to run with me. "Hurry. I need to find out what Jane knows about moving up."

I have to stop and get my breath after we reach her. She watches me while I huff. Then I ask. "Is there anything I can do to get a position with more pay and out of the scullery? The heavy pots and scalding water are killing me."

"Well, the workhouse is the only place I seen them choose staff by lining up girls." She says with scorn. "Most often, you have a letter, if possible, from the last place you worked. If not, you get several folks from the local town who know you and your family well. They need to say that you are of high moral character and a hard worker."

"What does high moral character mean?"

"That you are a good girl, you don't do anything improper with men or boys and you won't steal the silverware. That sort of thing. They really don't want anyone who has had a baby—with or without being married, but especially without."

"Oh," I say. I am thinking about the nice old woman and her son James, my uncle. "So, if a man has had his way with you, you cannot get a job."

"Yes. Sometimes even if it looks like you might be talking to a man. It is unfair. Sometimes the girl can't say no, but there it is. If she gets found out, she gets sent to the Magdalene Asylum to do laundry for the rest of her life. Nothing happens to him of course." She stops, lowers her head, and scrunches her eyes closed.

Then she takes a deep breath. "My favorite sister was cornered. None of it was her fault. When she started to get big, it all came out. There was no arguing. We cried, and I tried to hold on to her.

I still am furious when I think of my Da pushing her up onto a cart." Annie gets tears in her eyes at that. "Then he turned on my baby sister and me. 'She's brought shame on us and our whole town. Stop that caterwauling or I'll give you something to cry about.'"

"I am so sorry." I understand even better, now, how fortunate my grandmother and Mama were to have a home.

Just then I see James. I took a big chance talking to Liam in the market. I stare straight ahead, like I do not see him. I want to ask him about the brooch.

He looks away quickly. I don't think it means anything about the brooch, or does it? Now, he knows I am here.

Back to the manor and back to work, cleaning pots, heating water, polishing every surface in the kitchen and the scullery. Cook no longer smells like tobacco smoke. I am black and blue from her use of whatever is at hand to hit me. I try to be far away when she has the rolling pin.

The day finished, I drag myself to my room. Without getting undressed, I fall onto my pallet and sleep. I hear a giant stomping in my dreams. My door bangs open. I am fully awake, and she is over me. She hits me first with a skillet and when it flies out of her hand with her fist.

My scream sounds like a rabbit's, high and shrill.

She looks at me, then suddenly stops, picks up the skillet and leaves.

I need to figure out if I can block the door. I think she was sleep walking.

The only place I feel safe, now, is at vespers services in the small chapel. We go every evening. The master is of the Church of England. His lady is not. The servants, except those from England are Roman Catholic like she is. I wish she would get to choose, but vespers are always from the Anglican Prayer Book. The lady's eyes look like flames during the service as if she wants to object but has been warned or worse.

I have heard the master hitting her, but I know we are not supposed to know. I never talk about it. The day after I hear something, she always wears a black veil over her face in chapel.

First thing this morning, Cook announces to me, "We have our day out in two days."

I smile, grab her hands, and spin her around.

"What are you doing girl!" She shakes my hands away. Then the realization she will have a chance to smoke again must have hit her, because she grabs hold of me and continues to spin until we both fall, laughing, to the floor.

162

Friday morning and everyone laughs and talks. For once Cook is not even complaining. The footman in high spirits makes kissing noises behind us. Annie and I put our heads together like he doesn't exist. I want to break out in dance, but I now try to act more like a housemaid and less like a scullery maid.

I tell Annie, "When it comes time to be picked for a new position, I want to move to housemaid. I know I could if they gave me a chance."

She laughs at me. "You have become very uppity lately."

I say, "Yes, I am working toward being a Duchess afterwards." The whole staff laughs, including me, but in my heart of hearts I know I am royalty.

There is a fine mist, a day perfect to my taste. We spend the time singing songs in the Gaelic as we walk. We would be in trouble if anyone else knew what the words meant.

The market is the same as last time, except Liam and I don't talk much. Bored, I wander around the shop. Then I spot them. The walls are papered with posters of packet boats from Belfast to Liverpool with prices, times, and dates. Passage is very cheap, so little I may be able to save enough from this job.

I motion for Annie to join me. "There it is! I can almost pay for one of the lowest fares! Maybe, I can leave for England before I have to go back to the workhouse. Then, instead of going back to the scullery, I'll be sailing for Liverpool."

Annie gives me a quick smile then wanders back to look at the ribbons.

I am lost in my thoughts about leaving Ireland, when I run into James, or maybe he runs into me. I almost fall. He catches me and says, "Excuse me." Then he disappears as quickly as he appeared.

In my room, I take off my pocket. Something stabs me. It is the brooch. It is wrapped in its green wool. He could have kept it and sold it. He and his mother need the money. He returned it!

I realize now, its value is more the history, and less the money. Am I a part of the hope the Irish will someday be able to rule ourselves again? I have known of the struggles since I first heard my Da teach the Gaelic. Now it comes to me, this brooch holds a part of his dream. Sadly, like grandmother told me, I may have to sell it.

I rewrap it carefully and decide to figure out how to protect the point so that I can keep it on me. What can I do when I am taken back to the workhouse?

The dread of going back to that place is filling me more as the end of the season approaches. I have to save it and me. I need to escape soon. I will have enough money, I think, to buy my passage to Liverpool, but will immediately need to get some work, or I may starve in England rather than in Ireland.

My healing knowledge which helped me so much when I was in the western parts of Ireland have no value in England. There are so many healers in this part of Ireland, but I have heard stories about healers in England being accused of witchcraft and burned.

Chapter 23:
Never Here Again

The housekeeper sits alone by the fire one evening doing some mending. I stand and wait for her to speak to me. I have learned everything I can about being a housemaid on my own.

She looks up from her work. "Did you have something you want to say to me?"

I gather all my courage. "Yes, can I have a word with you?"

"What is it, girl?"

"I was just wondering what I would need to do to become a housemaid. I listen to the lessons and I am sure I can do it."

She almost screeches, "You, impertinent little wench. Do you not understand your place in the world?" With that, she cuffs me across my cheek.

I also get a demerit. It's not fair!

As I trudge up the narrow stairs to my room. I feel defeated. No! If they will not do right by me, I have to get around it another way. I can write, but if I am going to write my own letter, I require writing materials, the master's seal, and sealing wax. Except for chapel, I am not even allowed into the upstairs. This will be hard. I would like to see exactly what to say in my letter. I will figure it out somehow. I fall asleep wondering, scratching absently from the bites from the bugs in my bedding.

Morning starts early here, I put the kettle on and add peat to the fire. Still thinking of the housekeeper, I feel mad like I used to when

Mama got crazy with the drink. I slam the pots around looking for the one for porridge.

Cook comes after me with a ladle, and connects with my head and shoulders, then stomps into the kitchen. She did not get any tobacco for the second time and is out for blood.

Unless I get calmed down, I will not see tomorrow. I say my rosary, but God is beginning to feel farther and farther away.

Cook is in the hallway yelling at the housekeeper. At least it is not me. "My Lady is not satisfied with my plain cooking. She actually came into the kitchen the other day. 'No. No. No.' She says in her Italian accent. Everything is wrong to her, but she does not know how to tell me how to change the dishes, so she will like them. She just does not want what I make for her."

I, too, hate the mistress of our house even though I should pity her. She is as captive in this world as I am. She has no way of escaping. I would never want to be in a world where I lived in a strange place with strange foods and a man who hit me because he was not happy.

Whatever their problems I have to escape soon. I have finally figured out when I can get the paper and seal. Do I dare? I have to. I need to get into the master's study when he is beating her and find what I need and leave. Tonight, hopefully will be the night.

****

All has gone to plan so far. I am in the coat closet across from the master's study. I listen as people walk across the floor for the creaking boards. My back throbs from the heavy pots I washed earlier.

The slaps resound through the hallway. She sobs. "Oh mi amore. Don't you remember when we met?"

"Bitch!" I hear bones crunch.

She begs him, "I did nothing wrong. I just want it to be like it was before…"

Glass breaks. Is it a window?

This is my chance. I walk without a sound. At the door now. Slowly, I grasp the doorknob and…and nothing. The door is locked. I will not get into the room this way.

I hear the master yell, "Help us in here."

Then a door opens somewhere, and I start running to the back hallway and up the steps. I skip stairs so no one will hear them squeak. Here, I have to jump over several. I am so scared, I feel like I can fly over all of them if I have to. Just let me get back into my bed.

Made it. That way is never going to work. I had no idea the master locks the study. What can I do now? I should have thought of it. Everything from the food to the silverware is locked in this house. I bet his desk has a lock, too.

I shiver violently and pull my covers over my head. I can hear a great commotion downstairs for a long time. Finally, it stops.

I have to calm myself down enough to get some sleep. If I am too tired tomorrow, I will give myself away. Lord Jesus, Mary, and all the saints, please watch over me tonight. Please, help me to sleep. I breathe and start saying the rosary. God is here. I feel his peace then go into dreams of a new life.

The Lady does not go to the chapel in the evening anymore. Cook is still angry often, but no longer shouts so much. Something has changed.

I hear her muttering to herself as I reach the bottom of the stairs. "I told that stupid lady's maid to have her talk to O'Brian in Belfast. He would have fixed everything for the lady."

My O'Brian? Why would she need an herbalist? He used to send me on an errand every time a certain old woman would bring a younger one. Is it something like that?

I enter the kitchen and go to put the kettle on the fire. I want to ask Cook if I am right. One look at her tells me if I say a word, she'll have my head.

Cook says, "Tomorrow is the last time we will be going into the village."

As sorry as I am for all that has happened, I need to think about my plan. They do have paper and ink at the market. I can use a bird's feather cut into a pen like Da taught me. I have not yet figured out exactly how to seal it, but I will. First, I need to write the letter.

I have it! I will make it from the lady not the master. She is less well known and may not have an official seal yet or at least maybe hers is not well known. I will use the top of the brooch to impress the wax. We have some bee's wax in the kitchen for sealing the tops of jars. I can use a splinter used to light the peat fire to melt it.

As soon as we reach the market, I talk to Liam about my plan, despite the danger. "I have to have some paper that looks expensive and some ink. Can you help me? Please. My plan is to write a letter of reference and take it to England."

"I cannot just give you the paper, or the accounts won't be right. You will have to buy it."

It kills me to have to pay so much for the paper, but he shows me how to make an acceptable ink from lamp black. It will still leave me a little short on fare for the trip to Liverpool, but it is the only way I can get a job there.

I have heard stories from the girls at the workhouse. The fate of those who cannot find a job is grim. I have to have a letter of recommendation, or I will be one of them.

I practice on the dust in my room to make sure I can still write with my left hand. It takes a while to get it back to where it used to be.

The letter is written in my finest hand with all the proper swirls and the wording as close as I can get to what Jane remembered of one of hers. It was read in front of her. She doesn't read.

Done. Sealed with bee's wax, and ready to go. I have made a special pocket from a rag in the scullery. No one will feel it or the brooch. I will need to get away before we get to the workhouse.

My grandfather drives the wagon again. He does not feel like a relative, just a mean old man who hurts people. I am glad there was never a time we met while I worked at the manor.

Maybe he was sent on an errand away from the manor to torment horses or tenants while we were here. I am sorry I have any of his blood in me.

Once again, it seems like a very long way and I am stiff the one time he lets us out of the wagon. This time, even though it is the most uncomfortable place, when I return, I sit at the very back so that I can throw myself out of the wagon where the short span of soft turf is, right before we join the main road into Belfast. I can crawl over the back gate and drop down there.

I tell my friend, Jane, about my plan. The sounds of the wagon cover our conversation. She laughs at the part of the plan when I drop off the wagon. "Silly, we are not prisoners at the workhouse."

I sigh, "No, I am a prisoner. When I came here, they made me a ward. I have a guardian. I am so afraid. I know some orphan girls have been sent to the Magdalene's for just looking at boys. I have to get out of here before they think of me as anything but a little girl"

She looks me up and down and says, "You are right. You don't look like the child I first met. I will help you if I can. I came into the workhouse but since I am older, I can just leave. I was lucky to get a place. The rotten food, punishments and all were better than starving on the road."

We travel in silence for a long time. I am shocked. What I thought was a prison, is a place others were trying and failing to enter.

She is still awake, so I ask her a question that has been on my mind. "Why did you leave your last position? It sounded so much better than this one."

"If you must know, I only got this job because she did not ask carefully about my background when she selected us. I was a housemaid, and a good one, for a nice house in Belfast. The master was in shipping. But I made a horrible mistake. The young master there came home from the sea where he had been learning his father's business.

"I was young and had heard the rules but somehow I thought that it would not be a problem if he only paid attention to me when we were away from the house on my days off. So, while we were at the house, I would maintain strict adherence to the rules, never looked at him or spoke to him except to give short answers as required. He was the most handsome man. I dreamed of him night and day.

I thought we could get married and I would become the lady of the house and it would all be like a fairy tale. I would bring my family to live near us and we would be well fed and taken care of. That is not, of course, how it turned out."

She pauses for a while just staring into the gray of the sky. Finally, she shakes her head and resumes her story.

"He pursued me day and night both in the house and out of it. I was flattered by his attention. I imagined he was dreaming of me as much as I was of him. In the end, I did something that I am deeply ashamed of now and let him do too much with me."

"What do you mean by 'too much'?" I asked. I can tell she is embarrassed by the question, but I really need to know. I think Mama was supposed to tell me about men, but I have no mama now.

After hesitating, she says, "Well it has to do with having too many of his clothes and yours pushed aside."

I beg her to tell me more, but she does not say another word on that topic, so I ask her to go on with her story.

"In the end I got with child."

I know then, it is something like Da and Mama rustling under the covers late at night when they thought we were all asleep, but still I am not sure of what it is all about.

"After that I was considered unfit for service. I was fired immediately. No chance for any reference letter. My son is still at the workhouse, and I only get to see him once a week. I lied and said my husband died on the road, or we would have both been sent away. I want to get him out of there so much, but I did not make as much as I need to get both of us to Liverpool much less to America where I want to go.

"I pray the lessons from my experience will help you in your life. Hopefully my ideas for your letter of reference will find you a good position. I despair for my own life, and even thought of ending it all, but who would care for my little boy." She shakes her head. "I will figure something out."

I admit, "I had to spend some of my money on paper to make my letter. I am short just two pence for the trip to Liverpool. I have been trying and trying to figure out how I can get enough, I am sure when I get there, I can find a place and then make enough to emigrate to America."

She pulls some coins out of her pocket. "Here,' she says. "Take this as a loan and pay me back when you get your first pay at your new job."

"No, what if something goes wrong. I cannot take money from you and your boy."

"Take it, I need to know that someone can find her way. I can't tell you why but if you never give it back, it is important to me to know you are not stopped for the want of so little. I have lost so many of my own dreams, follow yours."

"Thank you, thank you. I will send it to the workhouse so even if you get away from there, check on it. I will get it back to you. I promise."

Once again, we ride in silence, but now I am thinking about other dreams. I am thinking of the dreams my grandmother had of me when she gave me the brooch. I think she was hoping that I would pass it on like a torch in a race until someone could bring the Kings of Ulster back to their glory.

I will not be that person, I am now sure I will be going to America. I am sorry that I cannot pursue her dreams and mine but that is not possible. One tear rolls down my cheek. It is for the grandmother who I knew so briefly.

Chapter 24:
I Can See It Now

My teeth chatter, the mist is cold. I walk quickly to the docks. I have my money and the brooch in my secret pocket tied around my leg under my dress. While I long to join the children gathered as they wait for their parents, I stare intently on the ticket line. I keep just behind a man with a broad back and huge arms. I want to give the impression I am with him.

We walk past the place with a sign for tickets. I duck inside and find myself in a room full of people standing in lines, then crouch in a corner to reach my money. My hands feel clammy, as I clutch it. The first lines are for America. How I wish I was able to stand in one of them. Next, are those going to Canada who are more wretched, the tickets cheaper. I hear it is because of the lower dock fees. Their babies do not cry, they just stare out with red eyes and snotty noses. The ticket sellers take their money and give them tickets.

The lowest class tickets to Canada are cheap, but still too much for me. A man in line grumbles to his mate, "Only water—little food for the lowest class. We need to find out how long they expect the trip to take so maybe we can scrounge food before we leave so it will last for the whole way."

I did not realize I would need food when I go across the ocean. I find the line for Liverpool. I have just enough to buy the passage. I am hungry because I did not go back to the workhouse. I could have left from there with food in my stomach, but no, I was right to not take the chance they might force me to stay.

The boat will not be leaving for nearly an hour. I decide to see if I can find the Catholic soup kitchen. I hear others talk like it is not too far from here. There is a Protestant one right across the road, but they make it clear the exchange is their soup for my soul.

It is farther than I thought. There are so many people, and it will take a while to get back to the docks. Even without eating, I might not make it back in time. My stomach groans, but I turn around. The smell of onion soup and bannocks pulls at me, so I run to get away.

Last call, I was right not to stay and eat. I guess I got used to eating regularly. With luck I can find a soup line in Liverpool, and a place to sleep.

My dress, the one from the workhouse, does not fit me very well. I have been growing over the summer. It is tight across my hips—which surprises me. I am getting more notice from men. It makes me feel like eels have taken up residence in my stomach where food should be.

As soon as we dock, I have to find a good road out of Liverpool. There are going to be a thousand people for every job offered in the city. My best chance is to find a place farther away.

I jostle my way onto the steamer. It stinks from the coal smoke. Da would have refused to board. For me, the crossing to England is boring. The stench of vomit from those not used to choppy seas hits me as I stand in the squeeze on the deck.

To keep from adding to the mess, I think of spinning the boys around in circles. I cry a few tears. I miss their laughs. The talk on board the ferry is mostly about the soup kitchen at this Catholic Church, St. Nicholas. When we reach the dock, the air is a little fresher. I breathe like I am gulping air.

My first view of England. The dock is very fancy, but filthy. After we go through the gates in the wall surrounding the dock area, I see most of the people are headed to the right. I hope it is the way to the soup line. The largest red brick buildings I've ever seen line the road. The door to where soup is served at St. Nicholas is not open yet when we reach it, but there are already many who are here before me.

"Yesterday, I was too far back and didn't get any food." one man says.

Another says, "It is all these damned Irish. I think we should throw them back in the sea and find out if they can swim."

I had thought I would ask questions, but people seem restless and I am afraid it might get me pushed out of the line or into the water. I stand silently waiting for my turn.

I finally make it to the front. I wish I had my own bowl like some of them do. Since I do not, I am given a bowl someone just got done with and then rinsed in slimy water. I do not think about it too carefully.

Once everyone has gotten some food the mood turns a little better. I ask a woman who sounds like she is Irish, where the best place to sleep is.

"I been sleeping under a bridge for a while, but last night there were a raid. They chased us away, beat my friend bloody. Not sure where I will sleep tonight."

The girl on the other side hears our conversation and joins it. "I found a garden near the city. It is not locked but I had to sneak in after dark and then get up very early to leave before the gardener came. I almost overslept and was lucky to get away."

I laugh, "I just worked as a scullery maid for several months. I wake up well before it gets light. I could make sure we get out of there before we get caught."

"Then, it is a deal. We will split up during the day. A group of us sulking around attracts the wrong kind of attention. You saw the windmill off to the left on the way out the gate?"

"Yes."

"We will meet there as it gets dark. I will take you to the garden. If you aren't there before moonrise, I will not wait for you no matter how early you wake."

I leave quickly. Here the wide street is crowded. A tall girl squats to do her business by a store. I would think nothing of it—back in Ireland. What else could we do with walls by most roads? But a man in a uniform waving a black stick rushes up. He hits her hard across the shoulders.

"You filthy scouse. Think you can get away pissing on the sidewalks here? Don't confuse Liverpool with your nasty Ireland."

I'm shocked. I was about to do so myself. I don't need to now.

The street is crowded with people, horses and carts. I start to walk down one street when the reek of blood and death hits me. I ask the girl walking beside me, "Why the horrible stench?"

She says "It is the Northside Hospital—the dying and dead do make it almost unbearable. Actually, I smell bad too. I volunteer there, and I cannot get it off of me no matter how hard I scrub."

It is making me gag. I leave her and avoid the whole area.

I duck down a street which is already filthy to relieve myself. While I squat, I notice a boy's body thrown on a pile of trash. I finish then run back to the main street as quickly as possible.

Finally, I come to a churchyard. There are fewer people here as it is much farther from the docks. There are nannies with their babies in big prams. I must not appear completely disrespectable, because when I sit on a bench next to one, she does not immediately get up and move.

"My mama was a nanny before she got married." I say. "I am hoping to go into service myself."

"Well, good luck around here. There are so many girls looking for work that there is little chance of it. Most girls who can't do better, end up in the trade," with this she gives an exaggerated wink.

I have little to no idea of what it is I am supposed to know,

"They be hawking their wares on the street. The ugly ones just starve or get beat to death. It is not a good life."

"Thank you for your help." I say and get up to leave. This is not good news. I hurry, as it is dark earlier than I had expected. I run to get back to the windmill. My new friend is still there.

I sigh with relief, then pant for a while. The other girl arrives, while I catch my breath. The one who knows where the garden is, introduces us, and we leave.

I had thought since we met so late, the place we were headed would be nearby. I was wrong. We walk in the dark at first. Then the moon breaks through the clouds. We pass the outer reaches of the city. The smell of the fields and trees are a relief. Finally, we pass a castle, and reach a long wall covered in leaves.

Our guide says, "This is owned by a rich sea captain. We will be his 'guests'. His garden is where we are going, if it is still unlocked."

The gate she shows us is almost completely hidden by vines. It squeaks and barely moves when we push our hardest. I think it could wake the dead or at least any guard dogs. But our leader is not concerned. With a jerk the gate gives way.

She leads us to a small shed by a large greenhouse. I have never seen a greenhouse, so she explains, "It is a place for things to grow when it is too cold outside."

I laugh, "I guess I need to live in a greenhouse."

"A greenhouse is for plants, silly," she snickers.

The shed which is next to the greenhouse has an unlocked door. It has a window and planting tables. Wood shavings are on the floor and tools line the walls. I take off my outer clothes and sleep in my shift even though the shavings are scratchy. I do not want to take any chances with the dress. I need to look as good as possible to get the position I desire, housemaid.

The next morning, I wake as usual before it gets light. The others do not want to get up but do. We get out of the gate with no signs of the gardener.

We are in no hurry to get back to the city. "The soup lines will not be formed until much later. Let's sit and rest by the road for a few minutes." The girl who lead us here says.

There are people starting to stir and it is fun to watch them. I try out the English accent I learned while I was with O'Brian on my new friends. They laugh, and one says, "You sound just like a native. You must have an ear for it."

"I hope it will help me get a job."

As we are sitting there, a young girl straggles past us towards the city. Her dress is too big, and her shoes are so large she trips over them. She is wiping her eyes and nose with her hem as she wails. "I only overslept a little. If they was just, they ought to dock me pay." With that she turned and glared at the castle with the garden where we stayed. "No, Mrs. High-and-mighty says I were to be let go. I have to help support me mum in Liverpool now Da is gone. That housemaid position weren't much, but now we will all starve, we will." She continues until we can no longer make out any of her words

I sympathize with her. "My da was hauled away by constables." I tell the girls with me. "As much as I am sorry for her, I think this might be my best and maybe only chance. I have to go back and at least try."

"We aren't going to wait for you. It's late and will be time for the line to form soon. Good luck."

I walk back to the servant's entrance. I can hear the housekeeper screaming. My heart hammers as I pull the string and wait. If I don't get this position, there will be no food today. After a minute, the big door opens, and a woman with white hair escaping her cap frowns down at me.

"I am here to apply for a job as housemaid." I say without hesitation and with my best English accent. I hand her my letter of reference.

"Well, bad news certainly travels fast."

Relief floods me when she ushers me into the servant's hall. She sits down at the table and puts on her glasses to read my letter. I do not sit. I know better. Instead I simply look forward without a word.

She reads carefully what I had written. "Why were you let go?"

Ready for the question I say, "I was working for a summer house in the north and was let go after the family went back to London."

She accepts my explanation, which was true even though the north I was talking about was in Ireland rather than England. I do not want to give her the idea I'm Irish. It certainly could not hurt to be taken for English.

"And why are you here?"

"I am on my way to Liverpool with hopes of taking a ferry south. I think my prospects might be better in London." So far so good, she does not even blink at that one.

While I stand in the hallway she talks with a man, probably the butler, in a nearby room.

"The lady has a headache this morning. It will be taking a chance, but we need to replace Betty now. We are already short."

He says, "This is quite extraordinary. You say she has a letter of reference? You're correct, it is worth the chance. Take her upstairs to get the Lady's approval, or it could mean both of our positions."

She whisks into the hall and says, "Follow me."

We go up the servant's stairs and down a long hallway with many doors then into the lady's dressing room. The lady's maid combs her long hair.

I only get the briefest of glances at the lady and her room. In all the time as a scullery maid, I was never allowed into a lady's room. I want to take in everything yet remind myself to keep my eyes to the floor. It is dark wood with a beautifully patterned rug. The heavy curtains block most of the light from the windows. The scent of her perfume almost gags me.

The housekeeper explains, "The newest housemaid, Betty, had to be fired as she was too lazy to get herself up in time to set the fires in the guest rooms. Unfortunately, we have a number of guests at this time and we are expecting more any day now. This girl comes with a reference. Normally I would spend more time checking it of course and will do so later, but I am inclined to recommend her."

I stand with my hands behind my back even though they look somewhat better since I have not been washing pots for over a week. Still they are rough and red, more like a scullery maid's than a housemaid's hands.

"Look at me girl." the lady orders.

I see a woman with a few wrinkles. She seems to be in deep pain. If I still had my herbs, I would fix her St. John's wort tea with willow bark and give her a lavender cream, but those are long since gone. I also see what looks like resignation. This lady has to do something, even if it is wrong.

"She'll do for now. If she steps out of line in any way, fire her. I am tired of servants who do not know or follow the rules. There are thousands where she came from so do not give her any slack."

We leave the room and I follow the housekeeper to the basement. "Ask Emma, the other housemaid, what the rules are. Be sure you follow them to the letter. I will send you with someone to show you your room. I think you are about the size of a previous maid. I will give you her uniform, you will still have to pay for it."

I say, "I understand."

Actually, I do not understand why I should have to pay for the clothes someone else has had her wages docked to get. Then to add to the insult, she had to leave them without so much as a single thread to sell to the clothing buyers. It is not my place to argue. Even feeling anger could lead me to do something, and they would let me go. Dear God, please help me now.

Her uniform does fit me reasonably well. However, I struggle into the corset. I hate it already. I can hardly breathe. The arms of the dress are a bit short for me. I am not a great seamstress, but I think I can let them out a bit if I can get a needle and thread. There is a generous amount of cloth.

I wonder how many girls like me have paid for these same clothes. I change in the washroom as there is no time to go to mine. The fires still need lit.

The housekeeper leads me to an upstairs hallway. She knocks on each door, apologizes for the inconvenience, and tells them, "Betty, here, will light the fires and clean your rooms from now on."

No anger, I tell myself at the sound of the new name. No anger.

Chapter 25:
A Chance

I have never actually set a fire before, only watched the process done while the maids at the first house learned. I have set it perfectly, I know. But when I try to light it, I get a cloud of smoke.

The guest, a young man, comes over and says, "You have never done this before have you?"

I shake my head a tiny bit. "You obviously have learned most of the process, but you failed to open the damper."

He reaches into the fireplace with the poker and pulls open the damper. The smoke leaves the room. "Now you do it. Feel up in here with the poker."

He holds my hand to guide it until I find it. I am both grateful and about to jump out of my skin. I have not read the rules yet, but I feel certain being in actual contact with one of the guests would be a good enough reason to be fired on my first day whether or not I know what is permissible. I am ready to jump into the fire to get away from him.

Maybe he remembers his place or mine and straightens quickly. "Sorry, I do not want to get you into trouble." I finish sweeping up around the hearth and quickly leave.

There are three more rooms, one contains an old man who frowns, his face red. "Why have you taken so long to get to my fireplace? My joints are stiff, and I will probably come down with the ague. Be sure to brush my coat. I need a valet. Can't they spare a single footman."

I understand he is impatient, but it is not with me, I just got here. He is in his dressing gown at a desk. His feet, from what I can see of them do look a bit blue. I resolve that from now on I will light the fire in this room first for as long as he is here. Today, it is perfect his room was the last. Thank you, God. As quickly and silently as possible, I light the fire, brush his coat, and leave.

This done, I reach down and pat my leg to reassure myself the brooch is in its place. Gone! I rush back to find the laundry room. I know I am supposed to meet the maid who is to instruct me, but the brooch must have fallen off when I was changing. I see someone coming and slip into the privy. If they find the brooch, they will assume I am a thief and fire me or just steal it. The sound of footsteps pass, and I breathe. What a stench. I hurry out.

The washer woman has her back turned to me and I am able to slip into where the clothes are and find my pocket, then dash back out.

The she hears me and calls out, "Who is there?"

I don't answer, just run.

The basement has a long table in one room and a small stove off to the side. It is not as warm as the rooms with the fireplaces but warmer than outside.

Finding only a lad, polishing shoes I hesitate. "I am to find the maid who will work with me. I was told she will instruct me on what to do today." He points to the room with light at the end of the hallway.

A girl with blue eyes and a pert smile is there. She introduces herself as Emma. The rules of the house are very much the same as in my last place.

"What about our free days? We used to get a day per fortnight."

"Those are some pretty fancy words there, Girlie. What is a

fortnight?"

"Sorry," I blush, no need in acting uppity. "Every other week."

She gives me a sideways grin. "Better. The days we have to ourselves are not every other week. They are more at the whim of the butler. He actually gets them from the Master of the house, so I should not be blaming him as he is only the messenger. The girl who got fired was working from well before dawn to midnight with me after one of those rare days. I guess she just could not take it and slept late one day. I know better. I will not be fired for such incompetence."

I ask, "How old was she? She seemed very young." "Well she was ten, after all, and had been in service for two years now. One would think that she would know better."

I think of Padraig. He was almost eight when he died. For sure he would have worked as hard as it took to keep the family going but he was almost a baby still. I was not working when I was eleven except to help Mama and Da. Maybe if there had been a place for me to get a job, I would have gone into service at eight.

"So, back to work." Her voice startles me out of the past and back to the present.

We spend the afternoon dusting the guests' rooms, making the beds, and generally cleaning every spot we can find to clean. I also am set to sorting and putting a nasty smelling spot remover on the laundry. I have to remember what each guest's clothing is so I can return it to the correct room without asking. Emma shows me a trick that she has devised. Near the hem or inside the sleeve she has sown a single thread of a different color for each guest.

****

As I try to go to sleep, Emma decides to explain who each of the current guests are. Of course, I want to know, but I wonder if the last

Betty's undoing was all this talk.

"I need to tell you about your responsibilities. You will be in the west wing of the house with the guests. The young man in the first room is Randall Goodwin, third son of a family in the south. He was in the army serving in Canada with the youngest son, Lloyd. They both shipped in here recently. He is expected to leave soon.

"The lady, Miss Grey, is the great aunt of the Master. It is not known how long she will stay. She is on the widow circuit of her relatives. They would just dump her if they could, but it would be a huge social gaff.

The older man Lord Hemphill, the gruff one, is a businessman. Sometimes his Scottish brogue is such he can't be understood so he yells louder."

I stifle a yawn. I need information, but sleep is even more important.

"The last guest is the Lady's best friend from London, Lady Westgate. She too is a widow. Her son has inherited all the property of course but she, so the rumor has it, has been given a generous annual stipend so I think she is only here to visit a short while then off for a trip to Egypt. She is not very fond of the cold and wants extra heat in her room all of the time. They have her in the east wing with family. In the oldest daughter's room, who is married and gone.

"I will be glad when the friend is gone, too. We won't have to carry extra coal to her room at all hours of the day and night. She stays up after the household has gone to bed and reads. I think it's what wore out the last 'Betty'. You will be expected to help with the coal in the night. Sorry.

I groan and rub my eyes. Is she blind? I need sleep.

"Anyway, there are three children, Anna who is married and gone. Arthur the older son and heir and Lloyd the younger son. I suspect that Lloyd will be going back into the army. There is really nothing here for him and he is expected to support himself. He and

Randall are both lieutenants and have aspirations of going higher. Of course, that depends on how much they can pay for commissions. I think Lloyd has good prospects, but I am not so sure for Randall."

We hear footsteps on the stairs. At last I can sleep.

****

I am still sleepy but up early as usual. I like the teatime for the servants here. At 9:00 am, an unusual time compared to every other place I've lived. It is a time for the butler, Mr. Alfred, and the housekeeper, Mrs. Gregg to relay orders that are special for the day.

Today it is about the upstairs ladies who have decided to go for a horse ride this afternoon. Emma will have to dress the Lady Westgate. It seems that there will always be more to do than time to get it done here.

I have enough to do to keep myself busy after lunch. Mrs. Gregg stops in to ask me if there are any questions on the rules and I assure her that I have learned them. Of course, I really have no idea as Emma could have forgotten half of them herself, but I do not want to seem like I do not know and more like I have been a housemaid all of my life. She leaves me with a few last minute things that need to be taken up to the auntie.

I run to get some tea from the scullery maid. I should learn her name as I have much sympathy for her position at the bottom.

The auntie is not feeling well and wants me to bring her a spot of brandy for her tea. She seems to be pleasant enough. Nods when I set down the tray and asks me to rub her back.

I would not like to be in her position of needing to hold a threat over my family just so they would take care of me. On second thought, my own grandmother did not invite me to live with her.

Today, as I am dusting, Russell's room, I notice a small plain book on the bedside table. It is Mary Somerville's book! The one

186

O'Brian and I were using for the experiment to set up the optics. There is a question I think I can answer. It has bothered me since the book was sold for the laudanum. Russell would not mind, I hope. I have to look.

As I have just about gotten to the part I want to read, the door opens. Russell steps in and seeing me, shuts the door quickly. I stare at him and then the book open in my hands. The book is back on the table and I wrench the door open and slip out before he has a chance to speak.

I race to my room and shut my door. My heart is trying to stab its way out of my body. How could I be so stupid? He can get me fired before I even get started! What was I thinking? I would stay here all day if I could. As soon as my breath slows, I go back upstairs and start dusting in an empty guest room.

****

The days have gotten predictably similar and it is beginning to feel like I have spent my whole life here. The only thing I am concerned about here, is the son's friend, Russell. He seems to figure out how to be in the room whenever I am.

He talks to me every time I enter. "Did you know my mother met Mary Somerville. I think she is a great lady. My mother taught me out of that book." Or, "I'm from Dover in the far south. Did you know that Mary Somerville was Scottish?"

I didn't know that, but I hold my head down and never respond. He hasn't told anyone of the incident with the book so far. I am just worried someone might overhear him. I don't think most young men would go on about Mary Somerville like he does.

I like when he talks about it. I want to ask him all sorts of questions. I didn't get to study it for as long as he did from what he has said.

No! I can't think about him or the book. My life is dependent on doing well here. My thought was, by just changing the order of when I go to each room, I could avoid him. No matter how I change it, he seems always to be there. I have to do my work.

Then, I thought maybe Emma could do the work in his room for a while, but she says that the schedule is set by Mrs. Gregg and it would be her hide if she did something different. It's true and I do not want to cost her the position.

Mrs. Gregg is sitting by the stove doing some mending when I come into the servant's hall. I stand by her until she looks up and asks, "is there something I can do for you?"

"I am sorry for bothering you, but I was wondering if you could change it, so I do not have to clean Master Russell's room. He is there every day when I come to start the fire and clean it. I have tried changing my times. I never encourage him by even looking at him. I do not want to get into any trouble with my position in this house, I was hoping that you could help me."

Mrs. Gregg looks at me for a few minutes. "No, Betty, I do not see how that can be done. Emma's work is in the opposite wing of the house and as much as I would like to help you, the lady has trained Emma to do things just so. I cannot have you trading. You will have to do better at discouraging him. Young gentlemen of his age can be a problem. However, I think you can handle everything."

"He has never done anything or said anything inappropriate, it is just that he is always there. I can feel his eyes on me as I try to get the work done as quickly as possible. I never look back."

I think to myself, maybe I should not have let him help me that first day. I know that I should have not let him touch me in any way. No! I did not let him touch me. He just did it. It is my neck, though, not his, if they suspect anything is going on. I have to figure this out.

Chapter 26:
Into Town

Everyone is starting to feel a little crazy from being confined in the house all the time. The butler, Mr. Alfred, finally says, "We are going to have a day in town on Thursday."

At my other position, when we went regularly, I never bought anything more than paper the one time. Still, I miss the open air and shops. This is the first time in several months we will get away from here. Mr. Alfred took care of posting my letter to Bonnie which was my only real task in town. Maybe Emma has something we could do together.

After breakfast I catch her attention before she goes upstairs. "Emma, I have seen so little of Liverpool. Would you show me around the market and any other interesting places?"

She hesitates, "I will do it, just this one time, mind you. My wages help support the family, and I don't want to be tempted. Still, it would be fun to wander around. It has been ages since I did. I won't get to see the boys and Mum. They will be there the next time."

"We could go to your place first if you want." I would like to get to know her family. She is so nice.

She hesitates even longer. "No, we will just look around the shops. I don't want to take up your time with them."

I don't know why she doesn't want me to meet them, but she can have her reasons.

Frank, the driver, takes the wagon for the trip to the marketplace in Liverpool. We sit on hay and cover our legs with warm blankets. The trees are beautiful all covered in snow. This is fun.

We make a stop out in the countryside before we reach Liverpool for a break to relieve ourselves. If only the snow was less deep. Still it is better than when we were with my grandfather, who did not give us enough chances to get out of the wagon and stretch our legs or take care of more urgent matters.

In town we stop at several places. Frank gets long strings of brightly colored beads needed for the Christmas tree and a special cake at the bakery. I don't spend any of my money at any of the places although some of the others do. It would be nice to have some sweets or my own little things, still, I remind myself I am saving to go to America.

We stroll around the market, smiling and shivering. Emma says she puts the old handbills she finds in the bottom of her shoes to keep her feet warmer. I like the idea, so we look for a post where there are some.

"Here is one for a masquerade at Vauxhall Gardens in September. There is another one for a summer concert there. Those are both from months ago." I grab the first and Emma gets the other one.

"It is good having you along." Emma says. "I have to take tattered ones, and then I am never sure if I will get in trouble for taking the wrong one. I wish I could read."

We keep them for later. It would not do to take our shoes off here with so many people even though my feet are freezing.

Even in the snow, the smell of chickens and hogs stink to high heavens so we get away from the animal pens quickly. I prefer the shops where we can feel the exotic rugs and look at the fine china. We don't look likely as customers, so we never stay in any one place for long.

My stomach growls as we pass a boy selling little meat pies on the street, but we brought the lunch the cook packed and will eat in the wagon on the way home. I hope we at least have hot tea.

I spot a little shop with jewelry and gold watches. There is a sign with three gold balls indicating a pawn broker down a side street. Next time, I may bring the brooch and see if I can sell it. There is a chance it might go back to Ireland, at least it could help me get to America. I have not told anyone I have it, and keep it hidden in my room. I do not want to have anyone find it by accident. That could be a mistake if I get fired suddenly. The garden might be better. I will move it as soon as we get to the manor.

When we get back to the wagon, everyone is smiling. Emma sits next to me as we bounce along. It feels like we are in our own little world here. We eat our lunch, drink hot cider, and, ignore the others as the wagon sways.

She talks about her family especially her brothers. They must be wonderful boys. They remind me of my own brothers. I feel tears forming so I swallow hard. "I have no family here." I say just to cut off her stories. "There is a chance my da is in America although he could be in Australia. I doubt I can find him either place but there is hope. I have heard so much about America on my trip. I dream of seeing it for myself.

"I don't know if the Americans have housemaids, but surely someone would need my help. I might even be able to use my healing skills when I get there. Maybe the people there are more open to it like they were in Enniskillen. There they don't even have a king. Just think of it."

When we reach the countryside, someone breaks out singing. One of our rules is we are not to let anyone see us being less than properly solemn. At first, I fear the driver will snitch on us, but he sings the loudest of anyone, so I join in on the song.

I hear the horse galloping towards us before Frank does. I quiet myself quickly and use my hands to hush the others. We are as silent as church mice by the time the horse gets to us. It is Russell. I don't know if I trust him on the matter of our singing or not. He never betrayed me yet.

He pulls on his reins, looks directly at me, and says, "Hello, Betty."

I want to hide under the blanket, but it would not be acceptable. "Good day." I say but I turn my eyes downward. I'm saved when Frank asks, "How are you today sir?"

Did he tell Russell where we would be and when? How else could he just happen to meet us here? He goes riding so seldom and the snow is deep.

"Oh, I am doing fine. I just had to get out on such a bright day to get some exercise and some for my horse. We have both been cooped up too long."

"I agree," says Frank, shading his eyes. "The day could not be brighter. Feel free to ride along with us back to the stables if you would like."

"No," Russell says, to my great relief. "I want to run him." He pats the horse's neck affectionately, "so I will get along now. So good to see you." He looks at me.

Frank answers anyway, "And good to see you, young sir."

As Russell leaves, I wonder if I can find a way to discourage him from speaking to me. It is hard when I cannot do anything but answer his direct questions, and then only to carry out my duties.

The rest of the trip back is uneventful, and we are excited to tell Mrs. Gregg all about it. Well, we tell all of it with the exception of the ride back. We don't share about laughing and singing or about Master Russell. She made it plain. I cannot expect her help with him.

Back to the sameness of my days, it's endless the amount of cleaning and mending that must be done for a house this large. The relief is that both the auntie and the businessman have gone on south. Neither was fond of the cold anyway. The expected company has not come yet, either.

The Lady's friend who was supposed to be going to Egypt is still here and so is Russell. Will he overstay his welcome? The Lady can have company for as long as she likes, but I have overheard the housekeeper complain to the butler about Lloyd's guest. She means Russell.

I have gotten used to Russell being in the room when I am there and pretend to ignore him. I gave up all hope he would leave me alone. In truth, he gets worse every day. What he says is interesting, but I fear he will get me fired.

****

We are going back into town in two more days!

It is finally time to get on the road. As Frank, the driver, helps us into the wagon, he says to each girl "My how lovely you are today," or "The frost is in the air, here have a blanket for your legs." His eyes sparkle.

As we settle into the back, Emma says, "He is to take me directly home and will pick me up there. Now, let's pretend we are a group of ladies on the town."

At first, I am just sorry Emma won't be with me, and barely hear the others excitedly talk about spending their money for Christmas presents. After a while, I shake off my disappointment and join in. "I hear they have oranges from Spain!" Maybe, I can smell them even if a single one would cost more than my savings.

We reach a dark and dangerous looking area of the city. There are clothes hung on lines between the buildings and the rats scurry between piles of trash. I am glad he does not let Emma walk here alone. When we get to a building that has black slime on the walls, I see little children without shoes or coats, who play with a dog in the icy road. I understand why she would not want me to see the inside if this is the outside.

Two bare-foot boys run up to the wagon. "Sally!" They shout, jump around, and wave their hands wildly. I don't know why I thought her name was Emma, mine is not Betty. I had just never thought about it with her. She jumps out of the wagon and hugs them both. Without a look back, they run into the dark ruin of a building. I am quite glad I am with the driver and the rest of the girls in the wagon.

He urges the horses on as fast as possible to get out of this area without hurting the many children in the way. I don't think he likes it any better than I do.

We get to a small tavern and he goes inside. I do not. I thought he was going to stay with us, but he must have other business. I also thought I would be with the other girls, but they quickly jump out of the wagon, brush off their skirts and are gone before I even realize it. I am trying to decide whether to follow the driver into the tavern or not when Russell appears. I stay in the wagon.

Russell greets me politely enough. "Good day, Betty."

"My name is not Betty. It is Mary"

He looks as surprised as I felt when her brothers called Emma, Sally. I do not know what made me say anything. I know my place, but I just wanted him to call me by my real name. I am so tired of having someone else's name. I want to go to America. I want things to be different. I want to be me.

"Good day, Mary"

"Good day." I have already said more than I meant to say. I look away from him, but peek back quickly.

He looks at me in a strange way. Does he want to say something? He makes a garbled noise, quickly turns his horse towards the tavern, and ties it to a post.

Is he crazed? He should take more care of my situation. I sit without moving until I hear him walk into the tavern. As the door closes, I sigh. I can breathe again, no longer afraid he will try to have a conversation with me here in such a public place.

My purpose here today, other than to enjoy the ride, is to take my brooch into the jeweler to see if I can sell it. I have no need of the brooch, and I keep thinking if I sell it someone from Ireland will see it and take it back there. I do not know why I am such a silly girl, but the thought that this is a part of a dream for freedom won't leave me. To sell it seems like throwing a bottle with a message into the sea.

I slowly unwrap the green wool to show the jeweler. He takes it and inspects it carefully. "Well, this is indeed a lovely piece, but I would not be able to give you extra for the workmanship. It is so obviously Irish and, I would only be able to send it to be melted down and sold for the metal value. I could give you half of that, I am a very honest broker, you are fortunate you came here. Many would not give you more than a quarter of what the metal is worth."

"You will not sell it as it is?" I cannot sell it to someone who will melt it. The brooch has to go back to Ireland. I cannot bring myself to let go of my grandmother's dreams. She entrusted it and them to me. I cannot do it even if it means my own dreams will take longer to reach. Just then, a bell rings and Russell walks into the shop. I quickly sweep it off the counter and fold it in its wool cocoon, but Russell has seen it. He knows my secret.

I nod to the jeweler. "I will have to think on it." Then push past Russell and slip out the door as quickly as I can.

Chapter 27:
Changes

This morning I wake with all sorts of fears. The knowledge Russell knows so many of my secrets is terrifying. I realize how precious my grandmother's brooch is to me. If he tells someone, I don't know how I can go on.

I wish I had other friends on the staff here besides Sally, I refuse to use her position name of Emma when I think of her. I am worried for her. She does not make very much here, and her family depends on it.

The other thing weighing on my mind is the fact that my references were not checked when I got my job. What if someone gets around to checking them and realizes that they are forged. I know it is enough to get me fired but what if I'm thrown in prison? I am afraid things may happen so quickly that I will have lost even the smallest chance of being on my own.

Back to Russell and what he tried to say. Why did he turn so red? Does he know that if the wrong person heard or saw him, I would probably be dismissed? It would not bode very well for him either.

They whisper downstairs about him overstaying his welcome already. Does he know that? The other concern I have is that he was in the jewelry shop. He did not come in quickly enough after my arrival to think he was following me. What is going on there? Is he not so well off as I had thought him? Yes, he is a guest in a fine house but maybe he is more of a freeloader than someone who is considered an asset.

After Sally gets back into the wagon. I tell her what he did when we were at the tavern.

She giggles. "He loves you."

Then grins when I ask, "What do you mean? He has made up a story about who I am." Does he even suspect that I am Irish and a Catholic to boot? He didn't even know my real name. I will continue to try to avoid him. I had thought there might be some innocent reason he was running into me all the time, but I think now he plans it.

I need to leave soon. I am good at my job. I get up before they expect so I can say my own prayers, and do not complain when the house has the required Protestant prayers later. I keep up on all my work and take on others extra if they need it without complaint or need for praise. I am doing my level best, but still I do not have any certainty that I will be allowed to stay.

At least I have saved all my wages since I started. I now have enough for passage to America and also enough that I will be able to live for a while before I get a job. I want to get one set of nice clothes. I believe many people would treat me better if I just had better clothes.

****

"Emma, I was cleaning in Anna's room the other day when you were so sick. They have kept her room just as she left it! She has been married and gone for a year now. She has a whole closet full of clothes she did not take with her or send for."

She says, "She had a whole new wardrobe made when she got married. I would love to have some of the beautiful dresses she had. I know that they are counted and cleaned four times a year."

197

I want to tell her I need to go to confession but not even Sally knows I am Catholic. I should not be coveting Anna's clothes. I also want to confess to taking the bee's wax from the kitchen. Also, I thought about stealing a sheet of paper and sealing wax. I need to find a priest.

Everything has moved much more quickly than I thought. Maybe the next time I am in town, I can go to confession while everyone else does whatever they do. I do not want anything on my conscience. I should also confess the forged letter. I will do that.

Mending finished, Sally and I leave for our separate duties. I need to dust the room where Russell stays.

As soon as I enter his room, Russell starts talking. "You know I was in the army with Lloyd, our unit went to the Americas."

I thought there was only the country of America.

"We were stationed in Canada which is still a part of the British Empire. It is also part of the American Continent. If I just say I went to America, then someone will say something about the United States of America. Do you know they don't hold allegiance to anyone there now?"

I wish the Irish had been able to do like they did, things might be different now.

As I dust, he continues. "My home is in Dover in the south of England. I miss it so much. It is a great deal warmer there this time of year. I used to fly kites off the great white cliffs and out over the English Channel as it got colder. On the other side of the English Channel is France, on really clear days my Father used to point it out. I miss those days with him. I went to public school in London and didn't get to see my father except on holiday. While I was there, I got top marks in penmanship and maths, he was very proud of me."

It bothers me he does not know how much learning I have. Of course, I cannot tell him about anything of my story. I am beginning to wish that I could. I would like for him to know that I am Irish and

Catholic and am possibly as good in maths as he is.

The next time I am cleaning, he continues. "We were stationed in the Canadian west. It was an exciting time there. The two halves of Canada had only been joined a few years before I got there. I will tell you that it was the coldest place I have ever lived by far. The nights were the worst with those icy winds from the north that would go right through the warmest coat like I was wearing the uniform meant for India. I have no heart to go back there which I will if I continue in the army.

"To stand guard there was considered punishment of the highest order so you can bet every shoe was polished and each 'i' was dotted."

I know I do not want to go to Canada, I want nothing of English rule and I certainly do not ever want to be cold like I was on that first night in the cemetery. I want to let him know that I have dreams of going to the United States. I hope there is somewhere there where it is not cold ever.

I am starting to think about Russell more. I am dying to tell Sally, but she doesn't know my background and I am afraid I would say too much if I got started. It has gotten so hard to keep my silence.

Today, he continues in his unending speech. "I have thought frequently of going to the United States. There is a city, New Orleans where they say it is much warmer than it is ever here. It belonged to the French but is now a part of the United States. I do not want to stop there for long but go on to Texas. There are lots of opportunities and lots of land open in Texas. It just joined the United States.

"The best is that they are starting to build a railroad there. I am just mad about machines and trains. I am sure I could get a job if I can just get there. The problem is the money. I have very little of my pay from the army left. Mostly I am living on an allowance that my brother who inherited everything is grudgingly sending to me. I have been living here trying to extend it while I decide if I could go to New Orleans or if I have to go back into the army."

I pretend to ignore his chatter, but this sounds exciting.

There is still the one problem that seems insurmountable to me. I am Catholic and he is a member in good standing of the Church of England. Could he just convert on the way to New Orleans? They have to have Catholics there if it was French. That would be so perfect. If he can't I will not marry him, and this dream is so much smoke out of Da's old pipe.

"Betty."

I startle from my thoughts. I hate that he is calling me that, but I know that it is for my safety more than his desired to call me by the wrong name. I still winced just a bit.

"I am going to have to leave here before very long."

I am so glad that he is leaving without being thrown out that I am startled by what he says next.

"I want to talk with you where you could talk back to me."

I almost break my silence to stop him from saying another word.

"I know if you got caught it could be bad for you. I am going to stay at the tavern. The one that you saw me that first time when I got so embarrassed. I was trying to tell you I love you."

At that I did glare at him. For him to say that here, for him to risk my position, I am more scared than really angry, but how dare he!

He lowers his head and looks at me sheepishly but does not stop talking. "I will be there for as long as it takes to see you again. I have an idea, but you may not agree with it. I just want for you to hear me out and to be able to say yes or no. If you do not want to go along with my idea, I will leave. I will go away and try to find my way to New Orleans or continue in the army before the last of my resources have been spent.

"We do not have to ever meet or see each other again. Because you might say no, I do not want to risk your position here. I think you are saving to do something. I see the other girls come back with small bundles of things and you never even go into the shops except that one time."

I blush remembering that I was trying to sell the brooch when he came into the jewelers.

For the rest of the day, I think about nothing but getting the tasks assigned to me finished. I also help the housekeeper with some mending. All she wants to talk about is small daily tasks. That's fine with me. I want the world to be right here for a while. Nothing is going to change if I am here. I do not want to think of him as a part of my future.

I am back in Russell's room when he starts talking. No surprise there. "I have written my family. Times are hard there also. We were never a very rich family. My brother Max has inherited everything so my only choice if I do not go someplace new is to go back in the army. It will certainly be Canada as I cannot buy a commission like Lloyd can. His uncle died and he has come into some money.

"I know the allowance that I am given will not support me. Also, there are so many things Max lords over me in terms of how I should conduct myself. I could easily get back into the army life. I have been on leave and I am not in disgrace, but I do not have the heart for it anymore. The things I saw were not about defending the country but more about making the lords and merchants even richer. I have done enough for them, I want to do something for me, for us, if you want to know the truth. But there, once again I am speaking too freely, especially here. You can tell the driver to find me in the tavern if you do not want to come into the tavern yourself."

The truth is, I have been in plenty of Irish pubs, especially before my Da had injured his foot. He would take me into pubs all the time and talk to the locals. He was looking to find fiddling jobs.

When I was really small Mama danced, too. I do not know why I should not want to go into this tavern.

The smell of those places carries so many memories. There were good ones of being on Da's knee but there were worse ones also. Even the good ones fill me with sorrow.

I don't know why I dare to take this chance, but I will meet him. Even though taverns are almost like home, I plan to send the driver in to get him, so I am not seen. I hope it is Frank since I can trust him.

Thankfully, the next day it is announced that we have a day in town. Russell just left the manor, we could have had to wait a long time. No one can see me talking to him. I might not want to go with him, and I have to keep my place here. I know where my next meal will be while I am here. I won't willingly go back to starving and sleeping on the edge of roads.

On the way into town Frank tells me Russell's plan softly so none of the others hear him. "Down the street from the pub there is a tiny old cemetery. There is no church or synagogue there now. No one ever goes there. I do not know whose people are buried there, but it is always empty. One of the stones is large enough for a person to be hidden from the street. Behind it are large bushes that cut it off from the houses behind it."

I think to myself, hopefully, he is right.

"Russell will be waiting behind the stone and you will sit on the bench in front." I hate the idea of being exposed at all but concede that it makes sense that we will not have to be seen in the cemetery at the same time.

"I will get him from the tavern. I will come back and tell you when he is ready."

I have serious doubts we can resolve our differences. The one thing I am most afraid will destroy everything is the question of religion. There are some other things that I want to work out with him before I agreed to anything.

I remember how it was strained in the manor house in Ireland. She resented it more each day when he forced her to bend to his religion. In the end the fact she was Catholic was part of what he would include in what he said as he beat her. Another thing, I will not be beaten by my husband. I have been on my own before now and I would rather starve to death than have that happen.

I do not want a man who can lose his temper over anything. Russell does not seem to be that type but how can I tell. I lost my dear da because he could not restrain himself. Our family was left without his help at the very time that we needed him because of his outburst. The surprising part was he seldom got angry at all. I doubt that I can have any guarantees, but I can tell him that the first time he hits me is the last.

I feel my own anger rising as hot as the sun. I had not realized I was so angry at my Da for doing what he did. I had always thought I understood. Well, I do understand, but it does not hurt me less to be deprived of his help because of a piece of wood with some strings. I wonder if he regrets his anger now.

The truth is things are changing whether I am ready or not. Even I am changing. I am having a harder and harder time keeping any of my own emotions in control. This was never the place I planned to stay forever. The slights of people who look right through me but demand complete obedience have started to wear on my mind. I have my dress now and all of the necessities for travel. If I cannot leave with Russell, I will have to leave soon without him. I have traveled by myself across Ireland and I can go by myself to America.

The next problem is the one of getting married. I cannot travel as his wife if I do not marry him and I will not travel with him any other way. What can I do? None of the Catholic priests would marry us because he is Protestant, the same is true for Anglican priests knowing I am Catholic. I will not start a life on that lie.

Oh yes, another thing, I do not even know if he realizes I am Irish. I have gotten so used to using my English way of speaking that he may not have any idea. I am not Betty the English housemaid. I am Mary McCarthy, the Irish orphan. Well at least that is something. I will not need to get the permission of my parents. No one here knows I am a ward of the state in Ireland.

His brother may object, however, if he does not approve of me. It would be bad if he withdraws Russell's allowance. He would probably want to meet me, and I am not so sure I could pass muster. Does he even know that Russell is thinking about emigrating to the United States? He might cut off his allowance if he emigrates so there is no guarantee he will get any money if I go or do not go with him.

Will there be enough time to settle all of these questions? I wish he were here in the wagon with me. We could talk about all of the things we both have been thinking. I smile. We could, and then the whole county would know that we are up to something.

Chapter 28:
A Sweet Boy

I do my best to look like I am just on a stroll through a quiet place. Still, I think my heartbeat sounds loud enough to be heard if I pass someone.

"Hello," I say as I settle myself onto the seat formed as part of the stone. This is a very old gravestone. Even though Frank has told me Russell would be waiting behind it, I feel like I am talking to the stones themselves.

"Hello."

I jump. I knew he was back there, so I don't know why I did not expect him to answer. It is not like I had wished it could be, with me behind the stone and him facing the street, but this will work. Frank said he would be here long before I arrived so we would not be seen together.

"I have bought us tickets on the Thomas B Wales. It leaves for New Orleans in a month."

I almost fall off my perch. "You have done what?" I am too shocked to remember to use my English accent.

He replies, "Betty, no, Mary, is it you?" I guess we are both surprised.

"Yes, it is, Betty or Mary; take your pick but I would prefer Mary"

Without warning, I start to laugh almost uncontrollably. It takes me a minute to stop laughing and when I succeed, he starts. Both of

205

us laugh some more. Tears roll down my face.

Deep breath. I regain control. "What on earth have you done, sweet boy? You do not even know me and, yet you have gotten tickets to New Orleans for us. And who, pray tell, did you say I was?"

"I told the agent I was booking passage for my wife and myself from Liverpool to New Orleans. I suppose he put you as Mrs. Russell Allen Goodwin."

"And you did all that without even talking to me first? You are an idiot, but I think it is the loveliest thing anyone has ever done for me." I take another breath. "I know you mean well but you don't even know—I am Irish and a Catholic to boot."

Now it is his turn to take a breath. "No, you never told me."

"Just when was I supposed to tell you with me not being able to say a word while you were telling me all of your hopes and dreams? I know you don't know me at all, but it is not my fault!"

I realize I had said this with a little more anger than I meant. "I'm not mad at you it is just we have a lot of things we needed to work out before we even started talking about tickets and New Orleans, and you have gone and booked our passage.

I like the idea of marrying you and leaving for New Orleans on the next ship over, but we need to figure out how or if we are going to do it. That is if you still want to marry me knowing I am Irish and Catholic."

He hesitates. My heart drops. It is the silence I have most feared since he started to talk with me. Is it a problem to him that I am Irish and Catholic?

As he hesitates my thoughts swirl. My da and his endless questions as he taught me about my land. Mama when she danced to his fiddle tunes. Sweet baby Bridie's coffin being lowered and Father saying words over her. The Sisters who took us in for a while. The Voice at the end of the road. Saying the Rosary with Mathair at night.

More and more, until he says, "Mary…Mary, are you still there?"

I startle at his voice. "Yes, I'm still here. Sorry"

It is not an issue to find you are Irish. You were born there and cannot change. The problem is you are Catholic."

Tears roll down my cheeks again, but not from laughter.

"Is there any way that you could see fit to change, to join the Church of England." He pleads.

I think very seriously for a while, "No. I cannot be a member of the Church of England. I was raised with too many stories of what was done to my family in the name of that church. I will not dishonor my family."

"Could you become Catholic?" I reply.

Without hesitation he says "No, but, since I do not know what the solution to this problem is, let's go forward, and just believe there is one."

I give him high marks for persistence. I like this quality in him, so I say, "I am listening. What other issues do you see we have, assuming we can get past that one?"

"Money, I spent almost all of the money I had on the tickets. I am sorry to disappoint you, but I am not a rich man."

"I figured out long ago you were not rich but were trying to extend your money by staying with your friend."

"You did? You knew?"

I laugh again. "I suspect everyone in the house had figured that one out by the time you left. Quite honestly, I was glad to see you leave on your own, rather than being shown the door. You cut it very close, I think. The downstairs staff were all taking bets on whether you would leave or be kicked to the curb. I refused to play. I think Frank won the bet."

"Oh. He is the one who finally convinced me I should leave.

And he did not even split his winnings with me. The fact is, he did me a great favor by convincing me my time there was soon to come to an end either way. I would have hated to be thrown out. My brother would have found out even as far away as he lives. He would have been mortified. I will have to thank Frank.

He hesitates a moment then says, "We still have the problem of money. I saw the brooch you were trying to pawn..."

"No. I was trying to sell it and decided against it. I did not sell it then, nor will I now. It was from my grandmother and contains her dreams for the rise of the Irish. I know it means nothing to you, but I have been living on dreams. Even though her dreams and mine have parted ways, I cannot stand the idea of having something saved so long and handed down so carefully to be carelessly thrown into a melting pot.

"The pawn shop owner told me the truth. I could go to someone else, but I know they would all do the same. No one here wants a fine piece of antique jewelry which is out of fashion and a symbol of a country they conquered, and the people who starve on their doorstep.

"I have thought about it for a long time, and I want to get it back to my grandmother to give to another of her children or grandchildren. It was the only thing she had to give me. I have the gift of the pride of the line of Ulster, therefore I must give the brooch back to her."

"Oh." It is all he says for a while.

I sigh deeply. I had thought about it for a long time but did not know how important it was until I spoke the words. Sadly, to take it back will cost money. I have so little to spare.

"Would you help me?" I do not think I should even ask it of him, but he had asked me to give up my church, so everything is on the table.

He sighs. I hope he knows this is a point he cannot win. After another silence, which seems to last forever, he says. "I understand. I want to propose a compromise. It will not get us the money we need but I think it may resolve our issues. I think I understand your ties to the life you had in Ireland."

I break in, "You can't know!"

"Wait," he stops me. "I know it is much bigger than I really know, but I am willing to listen to all you have to say, just later. I am willing for you to keep the practices of your Catholicism in your heart, but I cannot be married to a Catholic. I can't explain it to myself. I know it is true.

"When I was a soldier in Canada, there were some boys I met from New York in America. They told me they were called Episcopalians. It seems it is somehow an offshoot of the Church of England but after the Revolutionary War. They had deep problems with the idea of staying in the church of their enemy, also.

"Would you, could you, change to a church of similar practice but with the same issues regarding the Church of England as you have. In exchange, we would take the ferry to Ireland and take the brooch back to your grandmother, if you can pay for it. Sorry, it is the best I can do. Would it work for you?"

It is getting late. I need to get back to the wagon. I realize, I am ready to leave for America, whether I do it by myself or with Russell.

"This is too important to decide quickly. I am going back. My decision will be made in the next day or two. Keep your room at the tavern, and I will go there to give you my answer. There is one last problem. We are not married. I will not pretend just to stay together on the ship. If we can work out the rest, how can we resolve that problem?"

"I will think on it. When I see you again, I will have some solution. I understand the difficulty. We cannot be married in either church because neither would tolerate the other and we will not be able to change to the new church until we reach New Orleans. There has to be a solution though.

"Goodbye. I love you." Says the voice behind the stone.

"I love you too," I whisper so he cannot hear.

Chapter 29:
Decisions

Frank gives me a long look before he jumps up onto his seat and clucks to the horses. We take off. He is the one person who knows what I have been doing. I do not look back at him. I do not say a word the entire way to the manor. I feel like my heart is being torn into little pieces. Russell offered all I have wanted and more. I had hoped this could happen since I was in the workhouse without anything but a dream.

But at such a terrible cost. The Catholic Church has been my refuge. The Sisters saved us when we were first evicted. God has been with me on this trip. Saying the rosary every night kept the fear from destroying my mind.

The chance to take the brooch back to my grandmother. I could do it on my own, but Russell has given up the idea we would exchange it for money and even offered to go with me to return it. He was the one who said it was important and we could do it.

The other thing, the one about having peace in my house by having only one religion. I know how important it is. He did not say he was against my religion. Maybe he, too, is against the separation it would cause in our family. Otherwise, why would he say I can continue the things which have given me such comfort? I wish he could change and join me as a Catholic, but he cannot.

So, what are those things I would keep? I would continue with the rosary. I am not ready to give up my prayers for anyone. The other thing is if we would ever have enough money, I would want to send some each year to the sisters of the Poor Clares who helped us when no one else did at the first. If I could have those two, I believe I could stand it. This is breaking my heart.

My decision goes first one way then as positively the other. I want to sleep on it for at least one night. I look up to see if anyone has noticed me thinking. The rest of the girls are talking excitedly, it covers how quiet I am.

My desire to go to sleep soon, seems the only certainty. I still have to talk to Russell face to face, but it can wait. I eat the small meal, which is set out for us, I am always hungry, but I will not spend my money on food in town. I wish the rations which are barely enough could be increased. I should be thanking God for his bounty.

My prayers after saying the rosary, are for help in my decisions. Please give me the ease I need to finally get some rest. I am almost sure what He will want for me but not certain. Either way, I have to tell Russell. Whether I go with Russell or on my own, my life will change.

The sounds of the house wake me. I must have fallen to sleep in an instant. There are a few things which are certain now: It is time to quit my position here. I can take the brooch back to Grandmother now.

There are still doubts. First will I marry Russell or not? Next, can I break from my church? These are tearing me in two.

This time, a real reference letter is a priority. I have been good and honest, except for the letter. I do not think they ever tried to even contact my references, or maybe good things were said about me. I will probably never know. I must go downstairs now to talk with Mrs. Gregg.

She surprises me when I tell her I will be leaving. "I have thought you might go for a long time. I know young Russell was talking to you and I also know you were always proper around him. I had a young man like him once, but I failed the test, and I have had to work very hard to achieve this position in the manor."

I am startled to see her wink at me. And then she continues, "I married my young man."

"But you are here without a husband? I thought..." I sputter.

"I like to keep it this way. I went back into service at this manor when he went back to the army. It was really the only way we could save for our dream of having a little house and children. I knew we could live in one of the tenement apartments, but I did not want to raise my children there.

"He died fighting in Burma. I never saw him again. My mum kept my baby, but both died of the fever. I stayed here and worked my way up to housekeeper. I would have liked to be lady's maid, but my mistake cost me the opportunity. I doubt it will ever be something other than a wish, but I am well suited to being housekeeper. I will probably stay as long as they will keep me. Some dreams never do work out the way we intend, but God often finds something we did not intend. It is good, you know, if we do not make ourselves sour hoping for what did not happen.

"How much notice are you wanting to give? While a month is standard, we have been thinking of letting you or Emma go. The other guests have not come, and to save on expenses we have thought one of you would be let go soon anyway."

I am horrified to think Emma—no, Sally—with all those kids at her home would not have work. "I am ready any time. I would like to work until the end of the month, but Russell has bought tickets on a ship for New Orleans, and I want to visit my grandmother one last time." I do not add that I may not be leaving with Russell.

"I probably should not do this but accept it as a wedding present. You are getting married, aren't you?"

I say, "That is what the plans are."

"Then," she says, "I will make a gift from me to you of the pay for the last days of the month and a little extra to live on. It is not much but I have been saving almost all my money for years. I just never could get out of the habit after I heard my baby died."

I breathe a sigh of relief. "Thank you." I am so touched, my voice is a whisper.

"Also, I will make sure you get a good letter of reference. You have done a good job here and helped at a time I feared might turn into a disaster. Thank you."

I regain enough of my composure to say, "Thank you for all you have done."

"Oh, one last thing. The lady did write a letter to find out if your reference was in good order. I was so afraid we might find it was not, I threw it into the fire rather than posting it. You had proven yourself to me. I did not want to find out anything else."

"Thank you again, for everything you have done." I say. "I will go now to get my things and say goodbye to Emma. You know it is not her real name. Her real name is Sally."

"Yes, and I know your real name is Mary. Do you know mine is Ester Brown? Now, go ahead. I hope you do not mind walking back into town. Frank is already away for the day."

"Oh, I was hoping to say goodbye to him also. Please do so for me."

"Why of course or would you like to leave him a note?"

"Oh, could I? Does he read?" Immediately, I realize the trap I have walked into.

"I always thought it was you who wrote the reference letter. Most ladies do not use bees wax or a seal which looks quite so Irish."

The lump in my throat keeps me from saying anything.

Then she grins and says, "I can read it to him if he does not. I have no idea if he can."

I run upstairs and quickly get my things. I also take off the hateful corset which I was forced to wear. If I had my choice, I would never wear one of those again. I take a deep breath and smile.

Wearing my own clothes which are a little tight still feels wonderful, I go to tell the news to Sally. "I am leaving my position today. I am off to America. I hadn't thought it would be so soon."

I could talk with her for hours, but since I won't be here, she has extra work today. No time to share everything.

With tears shining her eyes, she smiles and says, "Thank you for everything but mostly my position. I know we do not have as many guests and one of us would soon be leaving. I was afraid it might be me."

"I will always regard you as a sister, Sally. You can trust Mrs. Gregg to read anything I write to you. I promise I will write when I reach a place where it is possible."

I go back down to the servant's hall to say goodbye to all who are there. Then, I turn quickly to leave before they see me cry.

I am my own person in a way I have not known before. I can support myself, and no one here knows I am a ward of the state. Yet, I might give up freedom to marry Russell. I know I want to but, in my heart, I think I cannot. With each step I am more certain I have to follow my God. I have cut my ties to the work which has sustained me, but I have enough to go to Ireland, then on to the United States by myself.

There is no one outside the tavern to get him this time. I walk in the door and see Russell across the room. The Voice speaks once more. I run to Russell and he looks at me. Tears are streaming down my face, I cannot even form words in my mind.

He holds my hand and waits. "If it is getting married, I have talked to the captain. He has said as soon as we get out past the territorial waters, he can perform the ceremony and he doesn't care if we are Zulus or Banshees. He swallows hard. Or, are you here to say no? Please do not let it be. We can work out anything else. Do not let no be your answer!"

I wipe my face and take a breath. "I came here certain it would be God's wish that I remain true to my faith. I opened the door with dread knowing I would have to tell you."

He is holding his breath.

"I heard the voice. The voice who saved me from dying after I fell at the false road. It told me, 'This is the man you are going to marry.'"

The End

Notes

Thanks to B. Sherrell for getting me started. I. Hudson for keeping me going, and to KCWG especially D. Souse and M.L. Kamberg and the members of Homer's Orphans for their sustained help.

A special thank you goes to The Ireland Writing Retreat with S. Hillen and all the participants who gave me a taste of the country I could not have gotten elsewhere.

My deep appreciation goes to the Linda Hall Library for their access to the achieved texts from Issac Newton, Émilie du Châtelet, and Mary Summerfield.

Thanks to Gordon Kessler, without whose help this book might never have been published.

The author may be emailed at: Libeth@Tempero.org

Disclaimer

The Great Potato famine was real. However, the novel while following the spirit of those times may have inaccuracies. The characters and events and places are strictly from the authors imagination. Any resemblance to anyone or anything, living or dead is coincidental. Nor is the timeline exact. All famous characters are intended to be represented as described by the characters and may not be historically correct.

www.ingramcontent.com/pod-product-compliance
Lightning Source LLC
Chambersburg PA
CBHW060142130626
46556CB00006B/2461